D.S. CRAIG

Reincarnated as a Familiar Volume 1

First published by Ranobe Press 2020

Copyright © 2020 by D.S. Craig

All rights reserved. No part of this publication may be reproduced, stored or transmitted in any form or by any means, electronic, mechanical, photocopying, recording, scanning, or otherwise without written permission from the publisher. It is illegal to copy this book, post it to a website, or distribute it by any other means without permission.

This novel is entirely a work of fiction. The names, characters and incidents portrayed in it are the work of the author's imagination. Any resemblance to actual persons, living or dead, events or localities is entirely coincidental.

D.S. Craig has no responsibility for the persistence or accuracy of URLs for external or third-party Internet Websites referred to in this publication and does not guarantee that any content on such Websites is, or will remain, accurate or appropriate.

First edition

Editing by Kendall Davis
Illustration by Yura's arts

This book was professionally typeset on Reedsy.
Find out more at reedsy.com

Contents

Acknowledgement	iv
Prologue	1
A New World	9
A New Life	24
What I Want	37
Training	50
Magic Circles	64
Growth and Relationships	77
Oliver	90
Ambush	102
Summoning	115
Despair and Vows	125
Results	136
Newsletter	146
Artist Information	147

Acknowledgement

Thank you to everyone who has provided me encouragement and support throughout this process, especially my friends and family. It was thanks to you that I was able to keep going even when the going was rough. An extra special thanks to my friend, Jesse. Thanks for listening to all my complaining, excited revelations, and other random outbursts. I wouldn't have been able to do this without you.

Prologue

For everyone else, it was the end of another long day. It was time for the kids to go home, but I still had work to do after this. There were assignments to grade, and I still needed to finish preparing my lessons for tomorrow. We'd run out of craft paper again, so I'd need to stop and get some more on the way home. It just never seemed to end. I honestly didn't understand how the other teachers manage. At only 23, and I could barely keep up. So much for youthful energy, I guess.

"Bye-bye, Ms. Williams!"

A shout from across the lawn snapped me out of my little pity party. I looked up to see Aiden, a boy from my class, waving enthusiastically to me. His bright smile stood in stark contrast to the battered brick facade of the school building and the weathered flagpole in the center of the lawn. I put on my best smile and waved back at the boy as he was tugged along by his mother towards their car. *Why can't you be this sweet during class, huh? You're always causing trouble whenever I take my eyes off of you,* I griped internally.

"Goodbye, Aiden."

Slowly but surely, Aiden and the rest of the students were all chaperoned away by their parents or loaded onto buses to be taken home. The other teachers and I were tasked with keeping the students from wandering off or getting into trouble. Our school didn't have enough money in the budget to afford additional staff for this sort of thing, so it was up to us to handle it.

I really wish we didn't have to spend so long seeing the students off. I still have so much work to do today. I turned and headed back into the school building to gather my things before heading home. With the hallways completely empty of students, it was much easier to see how run down the building was. The fluorescent lights dyed the hallway in an off-yellow color that was hard on the eyes. The only natural light came from the glass doorways at either end of the hall. The linoleum floor was noticeably discolored, and the white cinder block walls were scuffed here and there from the students' antics. If you didn't know any better, you might think that the students' decorations and drawings hung throughout the hallway were there to hide such marks.

I turned into a doorway about midway down the hallway and entered my classroom, only to be greeted with a giant mess. I immediately hung my head and pinched my brow just above the bridge of my nose. *That's right. I forgot that our writing class ran over today because Aiden kept distracting everyone. Why does he have to be such an attention seeker? Guess I'll have to clean this up by myself.* I set about cleaning up the various papers and writing utensils that were strewn about the classroom. By the time I finished and headed to my car, the sun had dipped low in the late afternoon sky.

* * *

I sat down at the small desk in my bedroom and pulled out the simple math homework the students had turned in that day. The cardboard remains of my frozen meal sat off to the side. It certainly wasn't the healthiest way to eat, but it was cheap and fast. The oversized T-shirt and shorts I wore were extremely comfortable and made me want to doze off even as I started grading.

The only sounds in the room were the gentle ticking of the small alarm clock on my desk, the pleasant humming of the ceiling fan's slow rotation, and the rustling of paper. The slight breeze caused by the ceiling fan had a wonderful cooling effect as it hit against my body, still slightly damp from the shower.

Grading was taking me longer than usual due to the high number of mistakes. I would take notes whenever I noticed a student struggling with a particular concept or problem, so it took me longer to finish grading on nights like tonight. *I wonder if my explanations were confusing? Everyone seemed*

PROLOGUE

to be doing fine in class. I wonder what happened. I began going back through the assignment to see if I could find any common patterns between each student's mistakes. By the time I finished, it was already quite late. *Ahhh, I did it again. I always get so engrossed in figuring out why they didn't understand a lesson, and I lose track of time. I still have my lesson planning to do. I really wish someone was around to stop me when I got like this.*

I wrapped up my lesson planning for the next day as quickly as I could and got ready for bed. By the time I was finished, my eyelids were so heavy I could barely keep them open. Normally, I would do a daily review before I went to bed, but I was just too exhausted today. I had already finished up all of my major work, so anything that I had forgotten couldn't be that important. I turned the light off and crawled into bed. I could already feel my consciousness fading as I pulled the covers up over me, and I was asleep before I knew it.

* * *

I woke up to the soft light of morning filtering through the curtains into my room and the occasional chirping of birds. It was the type of peaceful morning that would make you just want to lay in bed and never get up. *Why can't every morning be this lovely? I could just lay here all day if it weren't for work. I wonder how long I have till my alarm goes off.* I glanced over at the alarm clock on my desk. What I saw snapped my sleep fogged brain from its early morning reverie. It was already 6:30.

I leapt out of bed and frantically set about getting ready to leave. *I can't believe I forgot to set my alarm! The other teachers will never let me hear the end of it if I'm late this early on in the year.* I ran around my small apartment like a miniature tornado, tossing anything that wasn't absolutely necessary to the side. I finished preparing in a little under 15 minutes. *Okay, final check. Clothes, not a complete mess. Hair, passable, makeup...it'll have to do. Keys, graded papers, lesson plans, all check. Yes! All I need now is the cra...*

My heart sank through the floor. *I forgot to pick up the craft paper on the way home! What do I do? Can I get by without it for today? No, I definitely need it.*

Maybe I can borrow some from another teacher. Mrs. Robins usually has a good stock, but I really don't want to have to listen to one of her lectures. Grrr...I guess I don't have any other choice. I accepted my fate and rushed out to the car with my things.

* * *

I got to the school around 7 and hurried to drop my bag off in my classroom before heading over to Mrs. Robins' classroom. The first students wouldn't arrive for another 15 minutes, so the halls were still empty. Mrs. Robins' classroom was two doors down from my own. I paused briefly before turning the corner and took a deep breath, mentally preparing for the lecture that I was about to receive.

I peeked into the classroom to see Mrs. Robins calmly sitting at her desk, reading a book. She always got here super early and finished her prep work for the day well before any students arrived. *I wonder what she's always reading.*

"It's rude to stare," she said without looking up from her book. "Did you need something, Ms. Williams?"

"Sorry about that. I was just wondering what kind of books you were reading every morning. It must be interesting since you're always reading them while waiting for the students to get here."

She closed the book and slid it into one of the drawers in her desk. "Reading helps keep your mind sharp. It's part of our job as teachers to keep our minds in peak condition and reading is just one way to do that. You should try it yourself sometime."

Wasn't that last part a bit unnecessary!? She didn't even answer my question, and she threw in another mini lecture. Why does she have to lecture me about every little thing? I don't remember ever doing anything to deserve this kind of treatment. I just came to ask for some craft paper.

"I'll definitely have to try that sometime. Maybe you can recommend me something," I replied.

"I'll see if I can come up with anything, though I doubt I'll have read anything that will match your...tastes."

PROLOGUE

Ugh, another backhanded comment. She really must hate me. Why else would she say stuff like that? If I were tenured, I would totally let her have it! I put on a forced smile to avoid gritting my teeth.

"At any rate, what was it that you needed? The first students will be arriving soon, so you should be getting to your post."

She was right. I could hear the faint echo of the first few students who ate breakfast at the school filtering into the building. "Oh, right. Do you have any craft paper that I could borrow for my lesson today? I meant to pick some up on the way home yesterday but ended up forgetting. I promise I'll replace it."

"Is that all? Feel free to help yourself," she said as she waved her hand dismissively toward the stack of craft paper by the far wall. "Just make sure you replace it all by tomorrow. I have my own lessons to give after all."

I could really do without these backhanded comments. Anyway, let's grab what I need and get out of here. I quickly walked over and took what I needed for my lesson today. Tucking the papers under my arm, I turned to leave the classroom.

"Thank you, Mrs. Robins."

"Yes, not a problem," she replied in a bored voice.

* * *

"Why don't you try putting that piece here? " I asked.

"You think so?" replied the young girl as she stared intently at her half-finished collage.

It was early afternoon, and my class was working on a small art project. Each student was cutting up different colors of craft paper and gluing them together in the shape of a parrot. The classroom was littered with scraps of craft paper and smelled strongly of glue. The sound of the students enthusiastically showing off their creations filled the room. I was walking around the room, giving the students guidance here and there as well as making sure that they kept moving along at a good pace.

I won't let class run over today. The last thing I want is to be stuck cleaning up this mess on my own. Several of the students had fallen behind slightly for various reasons. Some of them would get distracted, and others would worry a little too much about getting every little detail just right. The little girl I was talking to just now was one of the latter. Fortunately, I knew her secret weak point.

"Yeah! Your parrot will look so pretty with pink feathers," I said.

"Really?... Okay!" she replied.

The girl set about gluing the pink strip to the wing of her parrot enthusiastically. *Yes! Another success. I think I'm on a roll.* I had managed to keep most of the students on track so far, and there were just a few more that I needed to worry about. *Alright. Let's see if we can get Mason on track next,* I thought, as I selected my next target.

"Ms. Williams! Ms. Williams!"

I heard a familiar shout from behind me and turned around to find Aiden standing there, holding his almost finished collage. "Aiden. What have I told you about getting out of your seat without permission?"

"I'm sorry...but I'm almost done, see? And I just need a little bit of blue to finish it, but I can't find any."

"Okay. I understand. Can you go back to your seat and wait for a few minutes? I need to check on a few of the others, and then I can help you look."

"Oh, okay."

Aiden returned to his desk, looking dejected. *Oh man. Why does he look like I just told him his pet died? I said I would help him in just a minute. I guess I should hurry up so I can help him.* I turned back and started checking on the last few students that were falling behind.

A few minutes later, while I was helping one of the other students, I noticed something was slightly off about the atmosphere of the classroom. The noise had died down a bit, and it was almost as if there was a slight tension in the air. I turned around and saw Aiden standing on top of his desk. He had moved it over to my supply cabinet and had climbed on top of it. He was tugging on some old construction paper I had forgotten was even up there that was wedged under a heavy box.

PROLOGUE

"Aiden! Get down from there! That's dangerous!" I shouted. I started walking swiftly across the room. He kept pulling on the paper, and every time he did, it would slide out just a little bit, bringing the box along with it. I reached the other side of the room as he gave one last forceful tug. I reached up and swiped Aiden off the desk and placed him on the floor.

I stared up at the now precariously placed box to make sure it wasn't going to fall. Once I was sure that the box wasn't going anywhere, the dam of emotions that I had been holding back finally broke.

"What were you doing!? You could have been seriously hurt! How would I have explained it to your parents if that box had fallen on you? This is why it's so important to do as I say and stay in your seat!"

"I'm sorry. I just saw that there was blue paper and I thought I could get it without bothering you. I'm really sorry," he said. His head was hanging so low that his chin was touching his chest, and tears were forming in his eyes.

I let out a heavy sigh and patted him on the head. "It's okay. I forgive you, but we are going to have to talk to your mother about this when she comes to pick you up. For now, let's get your desk and chair back where they belong."

Aiden nodded and meekly grabbed his chair and took it back over to its proper place. Meanwhile, I turned around and picked up Aiden's desk with both hands and started to move it back. As I turned, though, I saw the box start to move as the tension that was holding it up finally gave out. With my hands full, the best I could do was try to move out of the way, but I was too slow, and the box struck me in the head. It wasn't heavy enough to do any serious damage, but it was enough to stun me and make me lose my balance. As I fell, I felt my head smack against the corner of the desk and then hit the floor hard, and the world went black.

* * *

Where am I? It's so dark. I was surrounded by a darkness blacker than night, and I couldn't see or even feel my own body. There was no sound or smell, either. *How did I get here?* The image of a box flashed through my mind. *Oh, that's right, that box fell on me, and I hit my head. Wait, I didn't die, did I!?*

There's no way, right? This has to be some kind of joke, I'm only 23. I tried to call out to see if anyone could hear me, but the words wouldn't come out. It was like I didn't have a mouth to move. *This is crap! What kind of way to die is that anyway!? A six-year-old and a box are what do me in? That's absurd!*

Having finally finished venting my anger to no one in particular, I started to reflect back on my life up until now. It had always been a rat race for me. Studying hard to get good grades so I could get into college and get a good job and live the American Dream. Instead, I just ended up alone, saddled with student debt, and working a job where nobody respected me. *Well, at least I don't have to worry about paying my bills now. Still, I do wish that I could have found a partner, someone who could have taken care of and supported me a bit. That would have been nice.*

Request Accepted. Searching for potential matches.

What was that? Who's there!?

Ten potential matches were found. Additional parameters required to finalize the request.

Parameters? What the heck are you talking about? Is this some kind of trick? Stop goofing around! I really don't like being messed with!

Confirmed. Additional filters have been applied. Two potential matches remain.

Oh, fine. Just ignore me. Not like I need to know what's going on anyway. I'll just assume that you're a magical disembodied voice. Yeah, magic sounds nice.

Additional request accepted. Request has been finalized. Commencing fulfillment.

Wait? What? What's happening? For the first time since I had ended up in this dark void, there was a light. It started out as a small pinprick, but as the seconds passed, it grew larger and brighter until my entire field of vision was filled.

A New World

Eventually, the light faded, and my vision slowly started to clear. I found myself in a rather dark room with only the light of a few candles keeping the darkness at bay. The room was made of large stones held together with mortar. It was filled with a variety of tools that sat on workbenches, some of them familiar and some that I had never seen before. The majority of the room was covered in a thick layer of dust and cobwebs. Beneath me, a large circle had been drawn with many complicated shapes, characters, and patterns filling it out. A simple wooden door stood as the only entrance to the room.

The only other resident of the room stood between me and the door. It was a young redheaded girl, maybe 12 or 13 years old. Her hair was held up in a ponytail, and she was wearing some sort of formal looking school uniform. She stared at me for a few seconds with wide eyes, almost like she couldn't believe what she was seeing. The shock wore off for her first, and she started jumping around.

"I did it! I did it! I can't believe it worked," she said, " Ah, I was so worried that this was going to blow up in my face. I mean, there were so few references that I could even use. This is nuts!" The girl continued to ramble on about her apparent success until I finally interrupted her.

"Um. Excuse me, little girl. There's a few questions that I'd like to ask you if you don't mind."

The girl snapped out of her reverie and snapped to attention like a soldier. "Oh, right. The ritual isn't complete. Sorry about that. I just got so excited when I saw you standing there that I couldn't contain myself. Let's continue, shall we?"

The girl seemed to be acting a bit more formally now, so I decided to take advantage of her new mood and get her to answer my questions. "Well, before that, I have a few questions that I'd like you to answer if you don't mind."

"A test of wits is it? Alright, go ahead. I can handle anything you throw at me!"

"Wits? Um, yeah…sure. Anyway, here's my first question. Why are you so friggin' huge!?" It had been bothering me since I had gotten here, but everything was just way too big. The tables, the chairs, the room itself, even the girl standing in front of me was like a giant child.

"What kind of question is that!? Don't you know you're not supposed to ask a lady about her weight? What a rude familiar!"

"I'm not talking about your weight! I couldn't care less about that. I'm talking about your height! Why are you so tall? In fact, why is everything in this room so big? Is this some kind of gag where you've got a hidden camera crew?"

"Huh? Well, I'm not even sure what that last thing you said meant, but I'm normal height, maybe even a bit short for my age. This room is normal-sized too."

"Normal? You're like six times my size. How is that normal? I should be a little bit taller than a young girl like you if anything."

"Um. I'm not really sure what you mean. I think it would be more unusual for a cat type familiar to be that large. Especially an Astral Cat like yourself."

Yep. That settles it. This girl is crazy. There's no other explanation. Why else would she think that she could have a conversation with a cat? I lowered my head and brought my hand up to my brow like I always did when something stressful happened, and what I saw made my stomach drop. Instead of my hand, I was greeted by a cat's paw covered in smooth silver fur. I stared at my paw in silence for a moment before proceeding to freak out. I attempted to spin around quickly to get a look at the rest of my body. This resulted in me immediately face planting as I tripped over my own four legs.

I quickly stood back up and began rubbing my throbbing nose as I tried to process what was happening. *Okay. Calm down. There has to be an explanation for all of this. This crazy girl seems to have somewhat of an understanding of what's going on. I'm not really sure I can trust her, but I don't really have any other options right now.* I looked up and found said girl now crouched down a few inches from my face with her head tilted to the side.

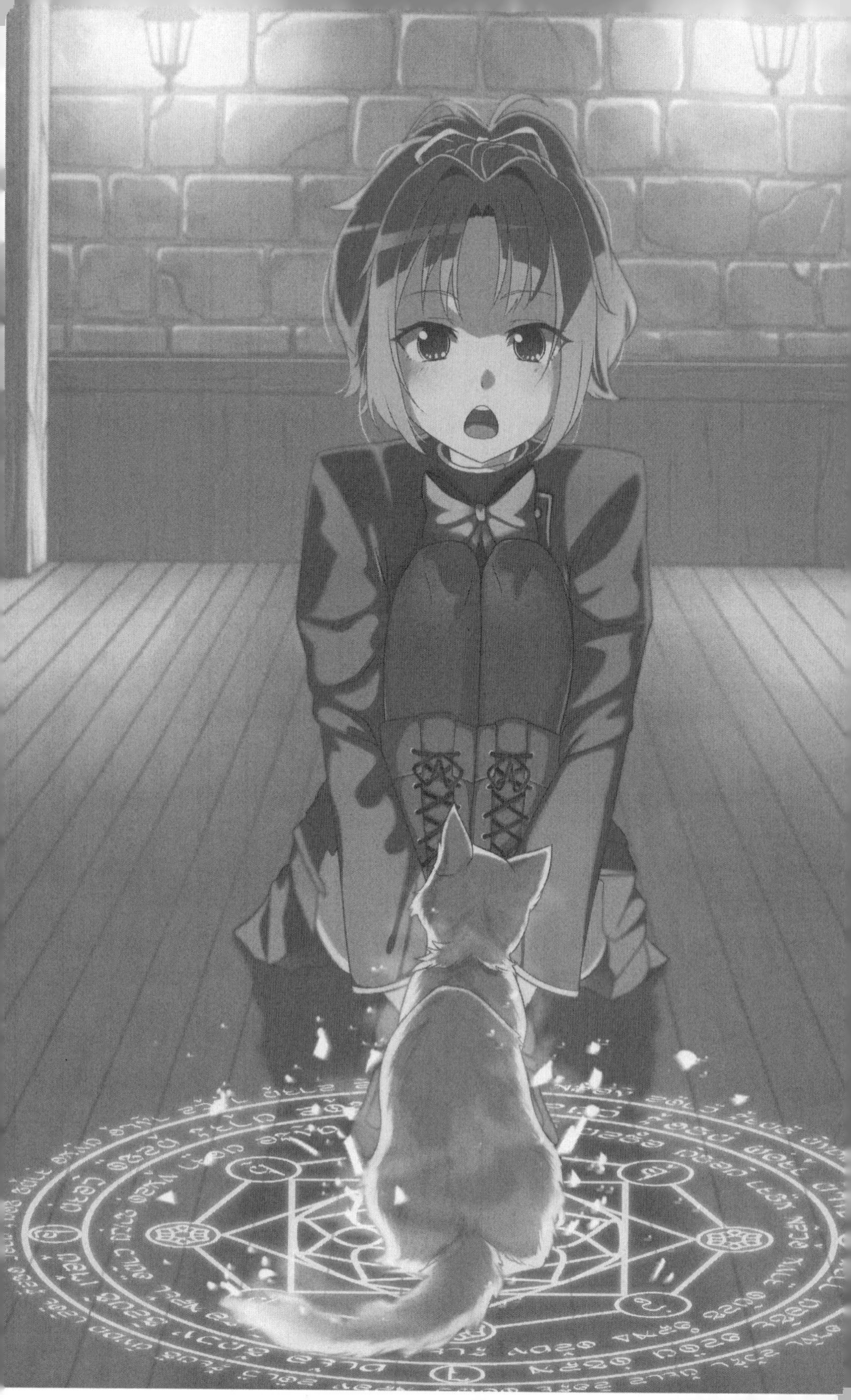

A NEW WORLD

"You sure are a strange Astral Cat, you know that?"

Give me a break! You'd be acting strange too if you were transformed into a cat and just dropped into a room with some random giant girl. I have no idea what's even going on here!

"Sorry, I'm just a little disoriented is all. I'd like to circle back to the "Astral Cat" thing in a second, but for now, let's just start over. Could you explain to me what's going on here…Sorry, what's your name?" I asked as I tried my best to get my emotions under control.

The girl jumped up and puffed up her chest out proudly. "I thought you would never ask! My name is Lesti Vilia, heir to House Vilia and future master mage. You can just call me Lesti, though, seeing as we'll be partners. How about you?"

"Oh, me? My name is…"

I tried to recall my own name, but for some odd reason, I was drawing blanks. I could remember almost everything about my life, even the faces of my family. However, I couldn't remember any names, not even my own. It was almost like it had been erased from my memories entirely.

"I'm sorry, but I can't seem to remember," I said.

"Hmmm. Then as your summoner, I'll have to give you a name," the girl said as she stopped to think for a moment, "I got it! I'll call you Astria. It's a great name, isn't it?"

"Astria, huh? Hey, wait. Are you just calling me that because I'm one of those Astral Cats you mentioned earlier?"

The girl glanced off to the side, avoiding meeting my gaze, as she replied, "N-no way! It's definitely a super original name that only I could come up with."

"Is that so? Well, it'll do for now, I guess. Anyway, ummm…Lesti, was it? What is this place? Where are we?"

"We're in the prestigious Alandrian Central Magic Academy, the premier academy for training up and coming mages within the Alandrian Alliance. To be more specific, we're in one of the old experiment labs. It's rarely used anymore."

"Wait. So, people here can use magic? I mean, I guess that makes sense given," I waved a paw generally towards my body and my surroundings, "Still, this is really hard to wrap my mind around. Although, maybe this is just because I hit my head so hard. Or I might be in shock. Does this sound like shock to you? I've only ever heard people in movies talk about someone being in shock. Do Astral Cats go into shock?"

"You truly are a strange one. I've never heard of a familiar who didn't know about magic before, especially not an Astral Cat. I can show you if you like, though."

"Really? Please do," I said. I was still dubious that my surroundings and my newfound cat-form were real and not the symptom of hitting my head, but I had to admit that I was excited. At this point, my inner child had taken over, and my imagination was running wild with possibilities of what Lesti and this magical world could bring to me.

"Alright! Prepare to be blown away by my incredible skills," Lesti said. She raised her hand in front of her, palm up, and began to chant, "Oh, fires of my burning soul, come forth and light the way forward. Dispel the darkness, guiding flames!" During the chant, I could sense a faint sort of energy gathering in Lesti's palm. When her chant finished, a small ball of fire appeared in her hand. The flame wasn't very large, about the size of a tennis ball and let off enough light that a person could see a few feet in front of them in the dark.

I frowned, peering up at the glowing orb. It wasn't nearly as flashy as I had expected, but I had to admit it was more than I could create on my own. As excited as I was to see magic for the first time, I was also a little disappointed by the lackluster display. Hesitantly, I cleared my throat.

"So this is magic, huh? Seems very inconvenient to have to use such a long chant for such a small light."

"Ugh...I'm not sure what you're talking about. This is a brilliant example of the guiding flames spell. I-I'm just holding back to make sure I don't catch anything on fire!"

"Is that so?" *I get the feeling that's a lie, but I guess it doesn't really matter.* "Anyway, if this is a magic school, then does that make you a student here?"

"Yes, that's right. I'm a second-year here at the school."

"And what exactly is a student doing performing a summoning ritual in a musty old abandoned classroom like this? Shouldn't there be a teacher here with you to make sure nothing goes wrong?"

"Ah! That's right! The ritual isn't complete yet. I almost forgot. We have to hurry!" she said as she ran over to a nearby desk and grabbed what looked like a small kitchen knife. She hurried back and took her place just inside the magic circle on the floor.

"Hey, wait a second! Aren't you going to tell me what's going on first!?"

"I'm sorry, but we don't have much time. I promise that I'll explain everything afterward."

Lesti closed her eyes and took a deep breath. After a moment, she opened her eyes and used the knife in her hand to prick her thumb. She held out her now bleeding hand and let the blood drip to the floor. As soon as the first drop hit the magic circle, I felt a wave of power take hold of me, and the circle began to glow faintly. It was like someone had turned the gravity up slightly just where I was standing. There was a sense of pressure that held me in place and prevented me from moving. I began to panic internally as Lesti started to speak.

"I, Lesti Vilia, do hereby swear my vow to you. I offer up my blood as a sacrifice so that I might borrow your power. In exchange, I promise to take care of you and keep you safe. I will show you a future that no one else in this world can or die trying! Grant me your power, Astria!"

Okay, this has gone far enough. What is she even talking about? She'll show me a future no one else can? Tiny, magic fireball or not, she's just a kid! As I railed against Lesti's vow internally, the power in the circle reached a crescendo, and a symbol began to form on the back of her hand. It was a faint silver color and resembled the shape of a cat, except the form was somewhat ethereal, almost of if it were made of clouds.

Just then, the door to the room flew open, revealing a young woman who was probably just a little younger than myself. She wore a uniform similar to Lesti's, but it was slightly more detailed and contained a mantle that wrapped snugly around her shoulders and ran down to her waist. She had straight, shoulder-length blond hair and a lean figure. A small glowing light floated just above her head out in the hallway, revealing her bright blue eyes, which were opened wide in shock.

"L-Lesti! W-What are you doing? This room is off-limits to students," she stuttered.

"Oh, hi, Lani! I was just...ummm...performing some extracurricular activities?" Lesti replied with an innocent smile.

"P-please, don't call me by that name. I'm your teacher, so you should call me Ms. Simon."

For sure, lady. Definitely the most important thing here. Let's worry about pleasantries and formalities when your student is in here summoning beings from another world in her down time.

"Aw, but Lani is so much cuter. Calling you by your family name just feels way too stiff. Besides, you don't call me by my family name like you do that rest of the students."

"T-that's beside the point, Les..Ms. Vilia. I'm your teacher, and you should use my family name when addressing me!"

Wow, she actually corrected herself. Lesti has this lady wrapped around her finger.

As this conversation unfolded, the light from the magic circle had faded, and Lesti had begun to wrap her thumb in a bandage to stop the bleeding. The power that had held me in place was also gone, so I assumed the ritual had ended.

"At any rate, what were you doing in this old classroom? Students are forbidden from leaving their rooms at this hour. I hope you weren't doing anything danger-"

As she spoke, Lani's eyes scanned the room until they locked onto me, standing in the middle of the magic circle.

"A f-familiar!? Lesti, what have you done? This is a serious violation of the school rules! They could expel you for this! What would you have done if something had gone wrong and you had been hurt?"

"You worry too much. There's no way that I could mess up such a simple spell, and since I succeeded, there's no way the school will kick me out. They can't afford to lose such a talented student after all," Lesti said with a smug look on her face.

I couldn't believe Lesti's guts. This was, after all, the same girl who was just moments ago super excited and surprised that her summoning spell even worked. She even got so distracted that she nearly didn't finish the ritual. I looked over at Lesti, who was nearly bursting with pride, and tossed a sympathetic glance over at Lani, who was looking more exasperated by the moment. Clearly this was not the first conversation like this for the two of them.

"It's not going to be that simple," Lani said, sighing. "Oh, I don't know why I'm bothering. You aren't going to listen to me anyway, are you? Come on, let's go. I'll be taking the both of you to see the headmistress."

* * *

Lani led us down the dark, empty hallway. The only sound was the echo of our footsteps on the stone floor. I hadn't been able to tell from inside the room, but it was the dead of night right now. The only lights came from the small magical orb that followed above Lani's head and the light of the moon that filtered in from the windows along the hallway.

I got distracted by the sight of the beautiful night sky and tripped over my own feet again, drawing a strange look from both of my companions. *Hey, don't look at me like that. I've been walking upright on two legs for over twenty years. You can't expect me to figure out how to walk with four legs in just a few minutes.* I stopped for a minute to take a look around without wounding my pride any further.

The stars were much brighter and more numerous than back at home. The night sky was absolutely filled to bursting with them. It was a breathtaking sight you could only normally see if you went out into the countryside. Between that and the light from the moon, I was able to see the surrounding area quite clearly despite it being so late.

The building we were in appeared to be an annex of some sort. The windows that lined the hall looked out over a courtyard with two similar-sized simple stone buildings on either side. Across the courtyard, there was an absolutely massive building that I assumed was the main school building.

It had an overall simple design; the main building was square with a tower on each corner. The building was probably three or four stories tall, with each of the towers about twice as tall. The exterior was covered in intricate stonework and large windows that were very similar to pictures I had seen of old Gothic-style castles. The aesthetic gave the building a slightly imposing look.

I drew a deep breath, trying to wrap my mind around my new surroundings. I was an Astral Cat—whatever that was—and I was the familiar of a little girl in magic school. Slowly, so as to not cause myself to stumble on my four legs again, I shook my head. Life and my memories before meeting Lesti felt very blurry, and even though my new reality was quite different from my past as a…was it a schoolteacher? Even though my present surroundings felt strange and frightening, I couldn't help feeling excited to learn more. With every step, this new reality felt more and more real than any fuzzy memory I still clung to.

Lani led us out of the annex building, and we headed across the large courtyard toward the main building. We passed through the first hallway and cut through another small courtyard in the center of the building, heading towards what appeared to be the front of the building. The large hallways were lined with classrooms. We eventually reached a room at the center of the second story of the front hall, which we entered.

The room was a rather spacious office. A neatly organized desk sat before a large window that looked out over the front lawn and gate of the school. From here, I could see for the first time that the school was inside a city of some sort. A tall brick wall surrounded the academy grounds. The office itself was lined with bookshelves on either side that contained large tomes. A couple of simple chairs were arranged before the desk.

"Wait here. I'm going to fetch the headmistress," Lani said as she turned and left the room. Her footsteps echoed down the hall as she hurried off to find the headmistress.

"So, what do we do now? It sounds like you're going to be in pretty big trouble," I said.

Lesti shrugged and plopped down in one of the chairs. "We wait. I knew I wouldn't be able to hide that I had summoned a familiar on my own for very long, so this was bound to happen eventually. Better to get it out of the way now if you ask me."

"I guess that's true. The mark on your hand is a dead giveaway after all."

All I got in response was a loud yawn. *I guess the adrenaline is starting to wear off. It is pretty late, so it's no surprise she's tired. I'm feeling pretty exhausted myself. I need to keep myself busy, or I might fall asleep myself. Let's take a look at these books, I guess.*

I began walking around the room and looking at the different books that lined the shelves. The spines were covered in characters that definitely weren't English, but somehow I could understand what they said. As my eyes glanced over them, the words just kind of popped into my head. Most of the books were covering various magic concepts, but a few seemed to be history books. One, in particular, caught my interest. *Alandria: A History of the Alliance.*

Alandria, huh? I've definitely never heard of any country like that on Earth. Am I on another world? Is that what happens when you die, they just zip you into another reality? Was that voice I heard then a god of some sort?

The sound of approaching footsteps cut my thoughts short. I returned to Lesti's side as she stood up. The door swung open, and an older woman entered the room, followed by Lani and another male teacher. The old woman had long silver hair pulled up into a bun and sharp green eyes. She carried herself with an authority that shouldn't be possible given the simple nightgown she was wearing.

The male teacher was a middle-aged man with short cut black hair with streaks of gray starting to show through. He had a strong muscular build that reminded me more of a warrior than a magic instructor. Each step he took carried a sense of weight and purpose the others lacked.

The three came to a stop inside the room, and the old woman's sharp gaze fell upon Lesti and me. Her gaze has such a piercing effect it felt like her eyes were boring a hole right through to my soul. *Uh oh, we might actually be in trouble here. These two aren't pushovers like Lani.*

"Frederick," she said, "Can you verify that the pact has been finalized?"

"Show me your hand, girl," the man said as he stepped towards Lesti.

Surprisingly, she held out her hand without a word. *I guess she knows better than to mess with these two.* Frederick reached out and took her hand. As he was inspecting the sigil on the back of her hand, I noticed that his own hand bore a similar sigil. However, his was black as night and shaped like the head of a fanged beast.

After a few moments, he released her hand and turned back to the others, "The pact has been sealed. It cannot be undone."

"I see. Then I guess we have no choice. Ms. Vilia, effective immediately, you are expelled from the Alandrian Central Magic Academy. Fre-"

"Headmistress Rena! Please reconsider," Lani interrupted, "I'll be the first to admit that Lesti did was reckless, but no one was hurt, and her summoning was even successful."

"Lania, I know that you and Ms. Vilia are close, but I cannot afford her special treatment. What she did endangered every student at this school."

Well, so much for her idea that they wouldn't expel her.

I looked over to see how Lesti was reacting to the news. Given the bravado she showed as we made our way to the office, I was surprised to see her pretty visibly upset. Actually, more than visibly upset. She was so upset it was almost a little frightening.

Her eyes were glued on the floor, and tears formed in their corners. She was clenching her fists so hard that her knuckles were turning white. A small trickle of blood appeared from biting her lip, and she was shaking slightly. Her expression wasn't one of anger, though, it was a look of fear and anxiety. Quite frankly, it was an expression that no child her age should have on their face.

"Um, excuse me. This may all be a bit over my head, but is what Lesti did really all that dangerous? She was in another building and-"

My attempt at reasoning with the headmistress was cut short by three shocked stares. Every single person in the room had turned to look at me with absolutely stunned expressions. Only the teary-eyed Lesti seemed unaffected.

"Um, is something the matter? You all look like you're rather surprised by something."

"Y-you can talk to us?" Lani finally managed to sputter out.

"Yeah. Of course I can, isn't that normal? Lesti didn't seem surprised when I first spoke to her."

The headmistress let out a rather large sigh. "Well, this just got much more complicated. Might I ask what you are called?"

For some odd reason, the headmistress had switched to a much more formal tone when she was addressing me. I frowned in confusion and glanced over at Lesti, who seemed to have shaken off the news of her expulsion and was just looking around rather confused now. *Well, since I can't remember what my real name is, I guess we'll just go with the name Lesti gave me for now.*

"You can call me Astria for the time being," I replied.

"Very well. Astria, you might not be aware of this fact, but most familiars can only communicate with their summoner. There are a few exceptions, however."

"And those would be?"

"The first is when the familiar is of the type that is normally capable of speech. This usually only applies to demons and the like. And the second is when the familiar possesses extraordinary magical strength. Dragons and other large magical beasts would be good examples."

"Well I'm guessing since Lesti's been calling me an Astral Cat, I would into the second category? Beings with lots of magic power?"

"Precisely. However, that in and of itself is unusual. Astral Cats aren't known to be especially strong familiars…"

The headmistress trailed off in thought. For a while, the room remained silent as everyone tried to process what was happening. Even I was at a loss for anything to say. I mean, it's not every day that someone tells you you're a super strong magic cat after all. Eventually, Lani seemed to steel her resolve. However, just as she started to speak, Frederick cut her off.

"Headmistress, I believe we should reconsider the girl's expulsion."

"Oh, and why is that? You're not going soft at your age, are you?" headmistress Rena replied.

"Perish the thought. I simply think it would be foolish to cast this little troublemaker out into the world when we know so little about the situation. We have no idea what her familiar can do and despite her...reputation here at the school, the girl did manage to complete a summoning ritual on her own. It would be better for us to keep them here, where we can keep a close watch on them."

"I see. You have a good point. Very well. Ms. Vilia, Astria, I will allow you to stay at the academy on two conditions. First, you are both banned from leaving the school grounds for any reason."

"Huh!? But how am I going to buy sweet-I mean supplies for my classes if I can't leave the school grounds," replied Lesti.

I nearly laughed out loud at how quickly Lesti turned from being devastated over her expulsion to worrying about buying sweets. We definitely would need to have a chat about priorities later.

"You should be able to obtain everything you need for classes on the grounds, and if there is anything that you need, then Lania can go and retrieve it on your behalf."

"Wait. Why do I have to do her shopping! I'm a teacher too!"

"And for my second condition…"

"P-please, don't ignore me," Lania said, feebly. However, the conversation continued to move forward.

"I want both of you to keep Astria's ability to speak with others a secret. That goes for you two as well," headmistress Rena said as she glanced at both Lani and Frederick.

"I don't have a problem with that, but there is an issue," I replied.

"And that would be?"

"I'm not sure how to communicate with Lesti without others hearing me."

"That's simple enough. You just need to think about directing your communications toward the girl only," Frederick said, "It's a similar concept to thinking without projecting your thoughts."

Alright, whatever that means. Let's give this a shot.

"Hey, Lesti, wave if you can hear me."

Lesti looked at me curiously but slowly raised her hand at me and waved. I looked at the rest of the group to see if they heard.

"I see you've already figured it out," headmistress Rena said, "Then, there shouldn't be any issues with my conditions, yes?"

"I'm fine with them," I said as I looked over at Lesti.

"It's not like I have another choice," she said as she shrugged, "I accept."

"A wise decision. Now, Lania, escort these two back to their room if you would. I'm going back to bed."

"Yes, Ma'am."

I don't remember much of the walk back to the dorms. As soon as the headmistress left, all the tension drained from my body. I was exhausted. So much had happened that I just couldn't process it all. As soon as we got back to the room, I jumped up onto Lesti's bed. I fell asleep almost instantly, filled with anxiety about what tomorrow would bring.

A New Life

The chirping of birds was my first indication it was morning. A single beam of light passed through the curtains onto my face, pulling me from my slumber. Despite the rather cool morning air, I wasn't cold at all. In fact, I was a bit warm. It felt as though I had been sleeping near a small space heater.

I lifted my head to look around the room and found the source of the heat. Lesti was sprawled out on the bed and had kicked the covers almost completely off. Her belly was exposed, and a line of drool ran from the corner of her mouth to the pillow. I had curled up next to her in the middle of the night without realizing it.

How is she not freezing? She's gonna catch a cold if she keeps sleeping like that. Makes a great heater, though.

I looked around the small room a bit more. I hadn't gotten much of a look last night, but the room was pretty barren. The walls and floor were the same rough stone as the room I had been summoned in. The only furniture in the room was a simple wooden desk, a standing closet, and the bed we had slept on. The desk sat on the opposite wall from the bed while the closet stood over by the door, opposite the window. There didn't seem to be any decorations, so the room felt more like a room at an inn than the room of a young girl.

As I took in the small space, I noticed that there was a lot of activity out in the hall. I could hear students talking as they headed to their morning classes. *Oh man, she totally overslept, didn't she? What am I going to do with this girl? It's just one thing after another with her.* I got up and stretched before trying to wake her up.

I put my paws on her exposed belly and started to push. "Hey, Lesti, come on. It's time to get up. You're going to be late. You don't want to get in any mo-," I trailed off as I became entranced by the squishy feeling under the pads of my paws.

Every time I would push, a pleasant, comforting sensation would pass over my body. I started to alternate which paw I was pushing with. Eventually, my claws started to come out a little bit without me trying. *W-what is this? It's so soothing! I can feel all of my tension just melting away! I could do this all da-.*

I froze. Lesti was awake and staring at me with an amused smirk on her face.

"Having fun?"

"N-not at all. I was just trying to wake you up," I replied as I averted my gaze, hiding my embarrassment.

"Right, right. I'm sure that's exactly what you were doing. Anyway, let's get going. We don't want to be late after last night. Lani is pretty scary when she's actually mad, you know."

She can actually get mad, huh? After last night, I just assumed she was some sort of saint. I sat on the bed and stretched while Lesti changed into her school uniform. She was done before I knew it and made for the door as she pulled her red hair up into a ponytail.

I hopped off the bed and followed Lesti out the door. We made our way out of the dorm building and headed across the lawn toward the main school building. The building we had just left was one of the two we had seen on our way to the main building last night. Based on the students leaving, one must be the girls' dorm, and the other must belong to the boys.

Now that the sun was out, I could see around the grounds much better. The leaves on the trees that were scattered around the grounds were various shades of red and yellow. Fall had already arrived in this area, apparently, which would explain why it was so chilly out.

We sure are getting a lot of looks. The entire walk was a bit uncomfortable. Everyone was staring at us and speaking in hushed whispers. *Looks like we're going to be the talk of the town today.*

I noticed that many of the older students had familiars of their own. They came in various shapes and sizes, but most seemed to be variations of normal animals. One boy passed by us with a large black owl on his shoulder. It was mostly normal except that it had a horn sticking out of its head.

The owl-like creature glued its eyes on me, staring at me like I was prey. Its large yellow eyes were boring a hole in me. That combined with the shift in perspective from becoming a cat left me feeling incredibly unsettled. I had never felt so small and vulnerable in all my life.

For a brief moment, I wanted nothing more than to be back in my old body. I felt my heartbeat begin to accelerate and my ears flattened against the top of my head instinctively. However, before my anxiety could get any worse, the owl flew away toward the roof of the building and I felt my body relax a little.

We eventually made our way into a large dining hall in the main building. There was a single wooden table where some women were serving what looked like vegetable soup and bread. Lesti grabbed a bowl of soup and two pieces of bread and made her way to an empty table. Most people had already eaten, so it wasn't too crowded.

Lesti broke off a piece of bread and dipped it in the soup before laying it on the table in front of me. I bit into the bread despite not being hungry. *Gah! My teeth. This bread is super tough. I see why she dipped it into the soup before giving it to me.*

"It's not very good, right?" Lesti said.

"That's one way to put it," I replied while making sure to direct my thoughts at Lesti, "I don't think I've ever eaten bread that was this hard before. Is this really all they have?"

"Unfortunately, yes. Breakfast is usually pretty bland, but the other meals are okay. Most of the more well-off nobles don't stay in the dorms, so the quality isn't too high."

"Speaking of nobles, didn't you say you were of House Villains or something like that when we met?"

"It's House Vilia! How could you get that wrong when the headmistress called me by my family name so many times last night?"

"Oh, my bad. You know, I guess it's just been a lot to take in. After all, I just woke up last night as an Astral Cat who apparently is incredibly magically powerful. But you're right, I should have remembered your family name." I rolled my eyes and smirked and Lesti, who shrugged and nodded. I continued,

"Anyway, you're a part of this House Vilia?"

"Yes that's right," she cleared her throat as she straightened up in her seat, "I'm the sole heir of House Vilia and its territories. Amazing, right?"

"Terribly. Shouldn't we hurry up and finish, though? We're the last ones left."

"Ah! We're gonna be late!"

Lesti scarfed down her bread and soup and returned her dishes to the cleaning station. We walked quickly through the halls and cut through the same inner courtyard we had passed through last night. However, we turned right this time instead of crossing over into the front of the school building. We quickly entered one of the classrooms that faced the inner courtyard.

The classroom was organized like a small college lecture hall. There were about five rows of desks, with each row sitting progressively higher than the last. A small stairway split desks down the middle. About twenty students were sitting around and chatting.

"Oh, Lesti. Done eating your slop with the rest of the rabble?" someone called out as we entered the classroom.

I looked over and found the culprit. A boy with sharp hawk-like eyes began walking towards us. He had shoulder-length black hair that was pulled back into a loose ponytail, which was draped over his shoulder. He had long bangs, which nearly covered his eyes. Overall, he had a rather wild look about him.

"Oh, my. Are we picking up strays now as well?" he said as he noticed me, his voice dripping with sarcasm, "That's so kind of you. Taking in a flea-ridden beast despite being so poor yourself."

Despite just taking on this new form, I felt incredibly offended. I was overcome with the urge to run right up him and give him a piece of my mind. But before I could do anything, I remembered my promise and stayed put.

"Astria is no stray, Sebastian. She's my familiar. I summoned her myself."

A murmur passed through the room at Lesti's declaration, and Sebastian stared at her with disbelief. After a moment, he burst out laughing.

"Oh, Lesti. Do you really expect me to believe that YOU, the lowest-ranked member of our class, managed to pull off a complicated summoning ritual all on your own?"

"Laugh while you can, Sebastian. With Astria on my side, I'll be taking the top spot in the class rankings from here on out. Starting today, I won't lose to any of you!"

I felt my stomach twinge in anxiety. Wasn't my entire existence, and any help I could offer, essentially just cheating? Why was she acting smug about using my power to get ahead? Besides, it didn't matter what her teachers said, I had no idea how to channel my powers. I didn't know the first thing about magic or being a familiar, and since I wasn't allowed to talk to anyone, it didn't look like I'd figure it out any time soon.

Sebastian clenched his fist, "What did you just say?"

It appeared I wasn't the only one that thought Lesti might be getting too full of herself. Sebastian was wearing an angry scowl on his face. The relaxed tone he had been using to insult Lesti was completely gone now, replaced by tones of hatred and resentment.

"You think you're better than me just because you found some mangy cat by the side of the road? Maybe I need to put you in your place."

The tension in the room became palpable at Sebastian's words. Everyone in the room was on edge, waiting for Sebastian's anger to boil over. Everyone except Lesti, that is. She stood her ground, her gaze level with Sebastian's. Her usual smug attitude was gone, but her expression told me that she wasn't planning on backing down.

"What are you all doing out of your seats? Class is about to start, you know."

A familiar voice came from the doorway. I turned to see Lani standing there with a tired expression on her face. She was wearing the same uniform as last night and had bags under her eyes from lack of sleep. In her arms, she was carrying a stack of books and materials that came up to her chin.

"Ah, Instructor Simon," Sebastian replied, " Lesti and I were just chatting about her mysterious new friend."

"I-I see. W-well, please take your seats for now. I'll be explaining that matter before today's lesson."

Is she intimidated by her own students? It's no wonder the other professors don't seem to respect her. The rest of the class moved to their respective seats, and Lesti took a seat in the front row near the center aisle. Lani walked over and sat her books and materials on the small desk at the front of the room and began sorting through them. She eventually pulled a rather large tome out and turned towards the class.

"Alright, I'm sure you all have noticed, but due to special circumstances, Lesti has formed a pact with a familiar. I know this is unusual, but the headmistress has given her blessing for the time being."

"Instructor Simon. Why is it that Lesti is allowed to have a familiar? Aren't students forbidden from bonding with a familiar until our third year?" a girl asked from the back of the classroom.

"W-well, as I said, there are special circumstances this time around. Unfortunately, that's all I can say on the matter right now."

A dissatisfied murmur passed through the room at Lani's explanation. The students didn't seem to be too happy that their classmate had gotten the jump on them without any good reason being given as to why. Lani quickly jumped into her lesson in an attempt to put an end to the griping.

"R-Right then. As you all are aware, the power and effectiveness of the spells we use is based on two things. First, our innate magical energy stores. Second, our ability to form a strong image of what the spell should be doing. While both can be trained, training the latter is much more efficient. So, for today, we'll be going over proper images and incantations to use for ice-based spells."

Well, that's interesting. So, mages have a limited amount of magic they can access. I would have just assumed that you could spam out spells as long as you want. I wonder what constitutes a strong image, though?

Lani continued her explanation of imaging and incantation techniques for ice-based spells. It was a bit long-winded, but the basic concept was simple enough. To be successful, the image you formed in your mind needed to be clear and as close to the result you wanted as possible. For example, if you wanted to use the attack spell Icicle, you would want to imagine icicles. However, if you wanted to use the Ice Wall spell, you would want to imagine a wall made out of ice.

It really does sound ridiculously simple. Basically, you just imagine what you want, right? I wonder why not everyone can use magic then. Is it because most people don't have a large enough pool of magic? I'll have to ask Lesti about that later.

"Alright then, let's have someone give a practical demonstration," Lani continued, "W-Would anyone like to volunteer?"

Lesti stood up and turned around to point at Sebastian with her usual smug look on her face. "Alright, Sebastian, time to show you what I can do now that I have Astria on my side! I'll show you the most amazing ice spell you've ever seen!"

There she goes again. Acting like she's queen of the world just because she has a familiar now. I haven't even agreed to help her yet, not that I would know how to do that anyway.

"A-alright, Ms. Vilia, please come to the front of the class and show us your best ice wall spell," Lani replied, "Make sure you have a strong image in mind just like we talked about."

Lesti walked to the front of the room and turned to face the class. She closed her eyes and focused. Then, after a moment, her eyes snapped open, and she held her hand out in front of her.

"Oh spirits of the frozen north, grant me your strength and form an impenetrable wall of ice before me. Ice wall!"

As Lesti recited her spell, I could very vaguely sense the magic power flowing from her hand. It seemed to be reaching out like it was trying to pull something that I couldn't see towards her. As her chant continued, a small wall of ice began to form at her feet. However, by the end of her incantation, it was easy to see that the spell had failed.

A small, poorly shaped block of ice sat before Lesti. The ice only came up to her knee and was already starting to melt. The so-called wall wouldn't provide any sort of defense in a regular fight, much less in a battle where your opponent was firing off spells of their own.

"Hahaha! Is that all you can do after all your bragging?" Sebastian heckled Lesti from the back of the room, "Well, I guess you weren't lying at least. That really is the most amazing ice spell I've ever seen."

Sebastian's taunt sent a wave of chuckling through the classroom. Lesti stared down at her sad excuse for an ice wall with a confused look on her face. Meanwhile, Lani looked on with a worried expression on her face. She quickly spoke up in what seemed like an attempt to cover for Lesti.

"N-Now, now. That was an excellent first attempt Ms. Vilia. Ice Wall is a very difficult spell to cast and even more so in a dry environment like the classroom. I wouldn't expect that many mages could make a full ice wall in these conditions. Keep working on your imaging, and you'll have it down in no time!"

Lesti returned to her seat without a word. The rest of the lesson went by without incident. Classes were dismissed a little before lunch, and students were given free time. The rest of the students filed out of the room along with Lani until only Lesti and I were left. She put her head down on the desk and hid her face.

She's taking it pretty hard. I guess I should say something. "Come on, it's not that big a deal. Lani even said that it's a hard spell."

"I just don't understand. I should have been able to do it with you on my side. I should be stronger now."

"Stronger? Stop messing around," I snapped, "You haven't done anything to get stronger. All you've done is try and use me without even asking me how I feel about it. Well, I have some news for you, Lesti. I'm not just some magical energy box, and I'm not just going to hand you my power if I even have any at all. You're going to have to earn your strength, your power through your own efforts."

I jumped off the desk and started to head for the door.

"I'm going to explore the school. I'll be back later."

Lesti never lifted her head or said a word as I left the room.

* * *

After leaving the classroom, I wandered through the school building in a counterclockwise direction. The general layout of the rooms was pretty easy to understand after I walked around for a bit. The hall where I started was on the left side of the building and contained nothing but classrooms and labs.

From there, I made my way to the front of the building. The first two floors were once again classrooms as well as a large entrance hall. The third floor appeared to be where all of the teachers' offices were. The one exception to this rule seemed to be Frederick. For some odd reason, his office was on the first floor of the tower that I passed through on my way to this hall.

I continued my journey into the next hall, starting with the third floor this time. As I wandered through, I saw a lot of what appeared to be small sitting rooms. There were quite a few students that were using these rooms for self-study at this time of day, though I didn't see any of the students from Lesti's class. Making my way down to the second floor, I found a large library that took up most of the floor. Despite its large size, it was filled to the brim with books on all sorts of subjects. It was again filled with students using their free time to study on their own.

As I was walking through the library, I heard the familiar voice of Sebastian conversing with another boy whose name I didn't know. They were on the other side of the shelf so I couldn't see them.

"Lesti really needs to learn her place," Sebastian said, "She's lucky to even be here with such low magical ability. Did you see that pathetic excuse for an ice wall?"

"Yeah, where does she get off acting so high and mighty? She probably would have failed out by now if it wasn't for the instructor always covering for her," the second boy replied.

"That pathetic excuse for an instructor certainly is a nuisance. No need to worry, though. We'll get to put Lesti in her place during the practical exams. By the time we're finished with her, she'll wish that she had failed out."

What a bunch of punks. I'll have to warn Lani to keep an eye on Sebastian and his group. I'll also talk to her about this practical exam, whatever that is.

I left the library and made my way to the last hall. The first floor contained the dining hall where we had eaten breakfast and a kitchen where the staff prepared meals for the students. The second and third floors appeared to be used for storage currently, so there wasn't much to see.

I was getting sick of the crowds of students wandering around the building. Being around so many people reminded me of how small and weak I was. I also had the feeling I was being watched. As I had wandered through the halls, it felt like there was constantly a pair of eyes on me, but whenever I turned to look, there was no one there.

So, I hopped up into the window of one of the abandoned rooms, keeping a close eye on the doorway. However, no one seemed to be following me in here. Eventually, I gave up and looked out over the lawn behind the main building. Several students were heading back toward the school building from the dorms.

I guess it's almost lunchtime. I'm not really hungry, and the sun from this window feels really nice. Maybe I'll just take a short nap here. I curled up in the windowsill and closed my eyes. The warmth of the sun and the silence of the empty hallway were comforting. Everything had been so crazy since I had arrived here that I hadn't had a chance to relax. My consciousness faded as the tension slowly bled from my body, and I quickly drifted off to sleep.

* * *

I awoke as a chill washed over my body. I opened my eyes and found that the sun had already set, and it was now dusk. The first stars had yet to emerge, but the chill of night had already started to take hold. I stood up and stretched before hopping down from the windowsill. I could hear the murmurs of conversation coming from the dining hall below me.

Whoa, is it dinner time already? Man, I really overslept. I wonder if Lesti is in the dining hall. I guess I should go find her. I was still upset with Lesti, but for the time being I didn't have anywhere else to go. Besides, despite what had happened, I didn't think she was a bad girl, and she was probably worried.

I walked down to the dining hall. The hallway was poorly lit, but I could still see fairly well. When I arrived, most of the students were on their way out of the dining hall. It was well lit, unlike the hallways. Small magical lights, similar to the one that had been following Lani around last night, floated around the hall. I looked around for Lesti but didn't see her. However, I did see Lani sitting on the far side of the hall.

I walked over and jumped up on the table next to her and privately said, "Hey, Lani. Have you seen Lesti anywhere?" Lani looked at me for a moment but then went back to eating her food without answering. She had a notebook and pen sitting next to her and started writing between bites of food.

What the heck. Is she ignoring me? What could she be working on that's so important? I looked down at the sheet of paper she was writing on.

"You aren't supposed to be talking to me."

Oh, right, I guess she can't respond to me without speaking out loud. "Sorry, my mistake. Can you just write down where I might find Lesti? I have no idea where to look." Lani started scribbling another message quickly.

"Lesti should be in one of the practice rooms on the second floor of the west wing. That's where she always is this time of night."

"Okay. Thank you, and sorry again. I'll be more careful in the future."

I jumped off the table and headed towards the second floor of the west wing. The halls were empty except for a few students and familiars that were running last-minute errands before bed. *I wonder what trouble that girl is getting up to this time.*

By the time I arrived in the hallway, it was completely dark out. The only light in the hall was the soft glow of a candle coming from a nearby classroom. I walked over and peaked into the classroom.

Lesti was standing there, hand outstretched. The single candle in the room illuminated her face. Her brow was drenched in sweat, and she was breathing heavily. A pile of quickly melting ice sat at her feet, surrounded by a small pool of water. A small plate of half-eaten food sat on the desk nearby.

Well, now I feel like a bit of a jerk. I thought she was just some lazy brat who wanted an easy way out, but she's practicing this hard every night.

"Another failure," Lesti began talking to herself, "I'm using the imaging techniques that Lani went over in the lesson this morning. My chant isn't bad, either. I just don't get what I'm doing wrong. Well, standing here talking to myself won't change anything, so let's give it another shot!"

Lesti held her hand out in front of her, closed her eyes, and started her chant.

"Oh spirits of the frozen north, grant me a yo-"

In the middle of her chant, Lesti staggered backward and slumped against the nearby desk, sending the plate of half-eaten food tumbling to the floor.

"Hey! Are you alright!?" I shouted as I ran over to Lesti.

"A-Astria?" Lesti said weakly, "Thank goodness you came back. I'm so sorry for this morning. I ju-"

"You idiot! That doesn't matter right now. Look at you, you're a mess. Sit down before you collapse on me."

"I'll be fine if I just rest for a bit. I used a little too much magic energy is all. It's totally okay."

"It's not okay! What if you had fallen and hit your head!? You could have died!"

"O-Oh, come on, you're overreacting. A little bump on the head wouldn't kill me."

"Oh, it wouldn't!? Because that's how I died!"

"Huh? Died? Astria, you aren't making any sense."

"Stop questioning me and sit down right this instant young lady!"

"Y-Yes, Ma'am."

Lesti slowly slid down to the floor and sat with her back against the desk she had been leaning on. A tense silence took over. The moment stretched on for what seemed like forever as I tried to compose myself. Lesti stared at me with an anxious look on her face. The only sound was the occasional gust of wind rattling against the large windows.

"S-So, what's this about you dying? You look totally alive to me," Lesti said, breaking the silence.

I heaved a heavy sigh.

"I guess there's no point in trying to hide it now. You probably aren't going to believe this, but I was once a human just like you. I died in an accident and I guess I was reborn as your familiar."

I spent the next half hour or so explaining everything I remembered to

Lesti. The life that I had lived, the world that I have lived in, and how I had died. I told her everything. I had meant to keep some things secret, but once I started talking, it was like a dam that I had built in my heart burst. All the emotions that I hadn't been able to express up until now came racing to the surface. My frustration and regret from my past life, but most of all, my fear and anxiety at being thrown into this strange new world.

Lesti listened to everything without saying a word. Her expression didn't show any doubt or fear. Instead, her eyes were full of empathy and understanding. When I finished, she reached out, picked me up, and hugged me close. In a voice almost as soft as a whisper, she said, "It's going to be okay. I'm here for you now."

With those words, I felt the last bits of the wall I had built up in my heart crumble. I cried. I wailed at the frustrations of my own failures that I had held in for so long. I shed tears for the life that I had lost and the loved ones that I would never see again. I trembled at the unfairness of the universe, which had taken everything from me so easily. All the while, Lesti held me closely, patting my back gently.

What I Want

Lesti stood in the empty classroom with her eyes closed. Sweat dotted her brow, and her breathing was heavy. It was clear she was getting close to her limit. I sat on the desk and observed her practice via the flickering light of a candle. A week had passed since my little outburst in this very classroom. Since then, I had been accompanying Lesti to all of her practice sessions.

"Lesti, this is your last attempt for the night. Got it?"

"Yeah. I know," she replied without opening her eyes, "I'm just about at my limit anyway."

"You say that, but if I weren't here, you would keep going until you fell over again."

"Give me a break! That was one time. I haven't overworked myself since then, have I?"

"I suppose that's true. Though I still don't feel like I can take my eyes off you. Anyway, hurry up and finish. I'd like to get to bed at a decent hour tonight."

"You sound like an old woman," Lesti said under her breath.

"Did you say something, Lesti, dear?" I replied, extending my claws.

"N-nope. I was just going over my incantation. Here we go."

Lesti recited her incantation for the Ice Wall spell. I carefully observed the faint traces of magic that I could see flowing out from her hand. It reminded me of a squid's tentacles. After observing for a week, I had figured out that the magical energy was actually gathering water vapor from the air. The tentacles would reach out and grab the vapor from the air and pull it into the shape that Lesti was imagining.

The spell finished, and a small sloppy wall of ice sat before Lesti. It was clearly better than last week, but it still wouldn't be useful as a defense. The wall still only came up to just above her knee, and it was still melting rather quickly. Lesti let out a heavy sigh and walked over to sit at the desk I was sitting on.

"You aren't making much progress, huh?"

"Yeah. It's frustrating, but it's always been this way for me. No matter how much I practice, all of my spells are average at best."

"Why do you try so hard then? You're a noble, right? I figured you would be set up for life."

Lesti looked down with a conflicted expression on her face before lifting her gaze to meet mine.

"Alright, I guess it's time I told you. I summoned you because I wanted to be stronger, after all. I owe you at least that much," A distant look came over her face as she started her story, "My family controls a small territory near the sea. We've never been extremely rich and we're not very influential within the alliance. Two years ago, my parents were asked to send some of our forces to assist another lord. However, they didn't like the idea of sending our citizens to die for another noble."

"So, they refused to send troops, then?"

"No. The lord in question had sent us aid during a particularly bad harvest some years ago. On top of that, this particular lord is very influential within the alliance. He could have used his influence to convince the other lords to abandon trade with us. For a small territory like ours, that would be a death sentence. All of that made it difficult for my parents to refuse. They gathered up as many fighting age men as they could and set off to war."

"I'm surprised the people followed them. Trading food for putting your lives on the line seems like an awfully bad deal."

"My parents were very well-liked by the people. Many of the nobles within the alliance treat commoners as beneath them. They never once thought that way, though. They believed that the success and prosperity of our territory was thanks to our citizens. We never lived a very extravagant lifestyle, but we never wanted for anything either. The people provided for us, and we did our best to provide for them in return."

"Your parents sound like wonderful people. I would love to meet them someday."

"That... won't be possible," Lesti said as she turned her gaze away from me, looking out the window.

Oh no. I'm such an idiot. She was literally just talking about her parents going off to war. I guess that's her reason for wanting to get stronger.

"I'm sorry. I didn't realize..."

"That's okay," she said as she turned back to me, "I'm sure you guessed by my reaction, but my parents died in that conflict. They sacrificed themselves so that their troops could escape an ambush. When I learned of their deaths, I was devastated.

"Is that why you want to get stronger then? For revenge?"

She shook her head, "No. Unfortunately, that's not where the story ends. Do you know how inheritance works in the Alandrian Alliance?"

"I don't have a clue. In my old world's past, territories would be passed down from father to son."

"Oh, that's surprising. It's rather similar then. As you said, territories in the alliance are passed down from father to son in most cases. However, I'm my parents' only heir."

"So, did your territory fall into the hands of some nasty uncle or cousin then?"

"No," Lesti said while shaking her head, "However, my uncle is administrating my territory on my behalf until I come of age. Once that happens, I will be forced to marry, and my husband will become the new lord."

Oh no. If this is anything like the middle ages back home, then I know where this is going.

"If you don't mind me asking, what age is someone considered to be an adult in this world?"

"Fifteen years old."

That's what I thought. What the heck is wrong with people? Marrying off a fifteen-year-old girl is a crime!

"So, you want to get stronger because you don't want to be married off?"

"If it were only that, I wouldn't be so desperate. The man who is meant to be my husband is the real problem. He views the common people as beneath him and has a reputation as a womanizer."

"What the heck!? Why do you have to marry a scummy guy like that? I'm sure your uncle could find someone better."

"Unfortunately, my uncle has no say in the matter. In the case that the only heir to a territory is female, the council decides who will marry them by majority vote. Ah, the council is made up of representatives of each of the noble houses within the alliance. Usually, they send either the head of the house or a second son."

"That's awful. Why should a bunch of old men and their sons get to decide who you have to marry! You should be free to decide for yourself who you get to marry!"

Lesti stared at me with a shocked expression for a moment before bursting out laughing.

"Huh!? What? Did I say something strange? What's so funny!?"

"Ha~. I'm sorry. It's just, that's what you're worried about? The world you come from must really be different, Astria."

"What do you mean?"

"In this world, it's pretty common for women to be married off without any say in the matter. That's especially true for nobles like myself. Even if my parents hadn't passed away, they would have decided who my husband would be. They would have never chosen such a pathetic excuse for a man, though."

I guess she's right. Even on earth, arranged and political marriages were common for a long time. Still, that doesn't make it right!

"You're okay with this, then? With being married off to someone you don't even love?"

"Not a chance."

"Wait, really?"

"Surprised? I don't plan on playing along with the council's decision. The man that they chose isn't fit to take over my parents' territory. My people deserve better than that. That, and I want to marry someone of my own choosing. I want to be the master of my own fate. That's why I need to be stronger. I need the strength to defy the entirety of the alliance and overturn hundreds of years of tradition."

I stared at the girl in front of me for a moment, awestruck. *She's incredible. I'm supposed to be a teacher, an adult. Yet, here I am being outdone by a child. She's trying to find the strength to fight the entire world. And what have I been doing? Just going with the flow and feeling sorry for myself.*

"Stop looking so down," Lesti said, interrupting my thoughts, "You don't have to worry about me. I may have some pretty big obstacles in my way, but I'm going to blast through all of them!"

"Ah, sorry. I'm just feeling a bit pathetic is all. You're working so hard despite everything that's happened to you, yet I'm just scared of this new world and unsure of what to do with myself."

"Is that all?"

"What do you mean is that all!? I'm all torn up over this, you know!"

"What's there to be torn up about? Shouldn't you just do what you want? Think about it. This is your chance at a brand-new life! You can do anything you want and be whoever you want! Although, I guess being a cat does limit your options a bit."

"You really are a strange one, you know that? You summon me all the way here to be your familiar and then tell me I can do whatever I want. What the heck is that?"

"You're my familiar Astria, not my slave. I want your help, but I also want you to be happy. So, what do you want to do with your new life?"

I lowered my head in thought. Since I had arrived in this new world, I hadn't really considered what I wanted to do. I had just been going along with the flow. *What do I want to do? How am I supposed to answer that? I don't even know what I can do. Maybe that's my answer then...*

"Well, the first thing I'd like to do is learn more about myself. I don't even know what an Astral Cat is, and I know even less about familiars."

"Maybe you should go and talk to Instructor Frederick? He's scary, but he seemed rather knowledgeable about familiars."

"What makes you say that?"

"Remember when we were in the headmistress's office? He was the one who knew how you could talk to me privately. He wouldn't have known that if he wasn't knowledgeable about familiars."

This girl...she picked up on that despite being in such a state of shock. She really is full of surprises.

"You really are sharp, despite being terrible at magic."

"Hey! That last part was unnecessary!" Lesti replied, puffing her cheeks out.

"Sorry, sorry. I couldn't help but tease you a little. I'll go see Frederick tomorrow during the free study period then. Want to come with me?"

"I'll pass. I need to keep practicing if I ever want to master this spell. That and I can't really deal with Instructor Frederick."

"Alright, I'll catch up with you after lunch then. Now, let's get to bed. We're going to be busy tomorrow."

* * *

Well, this is a problem. It was the next day, and I was standing outside the closed door of Frederick's office. I stared up at the simple handle far above my head. *How am I supposed to open this? Maybe I can jump and grab the handle? Guess I'll give it a shot.* I quickly looked around to make sure that no one was watching before crouching down and getting ready to jump.

After a moment, I leapt up at the handle with my paws extended out in front of me. I managed to reach, but my paws slipped off the smooth surface, and I went tumbling to the floor. Right before I hit the ground, I managed to twist my body around and land on my feet. *Gah! Almost had it! Still, I am happy to learn that it's true what they say about cats always landing on their feet. I would have fallen right on my face as a human.*

I got back in position and crouched down. I once again leapt up at the handle, but this time I wrapped my front paws around it like I was giving it a hug. I then pulled my back paws up and braced them against the door to support myself. *Alright, I got it! Now all I need to do is-.* My thoughts were cut short by the sight of Frederick standing in the hall with an unimpressed look on his face.

"Having fun attacking my door?" he asked sarcastically.

Why does this keep happening to me! First, it was waking up Lesti and now this! I have got to be more careful where I let my cat-urges get the better of me.

I hopped down from the door handle and turned to face Frederick. I couldn't bring myself to meet his gaze, so I pretended to be fascinated with the nearby wall.

"I-I was just trying to see if you were around."

Frederick moved over and opened the door, inviting me inside. *Oh, right. He can't respond to me out here.* I went into his office, and he closed the door behind me.

"I would say you should knock next time, but I guess that's impossible," he said, "I'll make sure to leave my door cracked if I'm in my office from now on."

"Thanks. That'll really help me out."

"I assume you needed something from me?"

"Yes. I've been thinking it over, and I want to learn more about being a familiar." I started to ask about Astral Cats as well, but since I wasn't sure if I should let anyone other than Lesti know that I used to be human, I focused on my questions about being a familiar. "I don't understand what a familiar is capable of. Do I have special powers and abilities I should be able to use? I feel like I'm just a really smart cat right now."

"I see. And you thought I could help you?"

"Well, Lesti thought you might know something since you were the one who taught us how to communicate privately."

"A rather sound conclusion, considering it's coming from that girl. Unfortunately, I'm not an expert on familiars. However, I do know someone who should be able to help you. He's far older and wiser than I am."

"Really!? Is he a teacher here at the school? I figured that Lesti would know about someone like that." I replied as my tail swished back and forth in excitement.

"No. He isn't a teacher. He is an expert on familiars though…in a sense."

"Um, that last part has me a bit worried. I guess beggars can't be choosers, though. So, where can I meet this familiar expert of yours at? I hope you remember that I can't leave the school."

"Don't worry. He's technically on the school grounds, so you'll be able to meet him without breaking your promise. I can take you to him after lessons are finished today. Wait for me outside my office. And do try to avoid attacking my door this time, please."

"Okay, I wasn't attacking your door, guy."

Frederick raised an eyebrow, bemused. I stopped talking and shook my head.

"You know what? I don't need to explain myself to you. I'm leaving! Thanks for the information. I'll meet you here later today."

I tried to storm out of the room angrily, but the door was shut. I paused for a moment, trying to figure out how to open the door myself.

"Um, would you mind getting the door for me?"

Frederick walked over to the door and pulled it open wide before bowing with a flourish. Surprised at the exaggerated mockery, I stuck my tongue out at him and then turned and walked down the hallway to meet up with Lesti. The look of surprise on his face filled me with a sense of satisfaction the whole way.

* * *

It was after classes, and I was sitting outside Frederick's office. I arrived a little later than planned because I spent nearly thirty minutes trying to convince Lesti not to practice while I wasn't around. In the end, I was at least able to get her to promise me that she wouldn't overdo it.

Like I believe that. That girl doesn't know the meaning of taking it easy. I wish Frederick would hurry up. I need to get back before she goes and collapses on me again. Where could he be?

A few minutes later, I spotted Frederick walking down the hall. He was walking with a boy I had never seen before. He looked to be about the same age as Lesti and had short blond hair that was neatly styled. His blue eyes were sharp, and he carried himself with an air that didn't match his young face. Most shocking, though, was the magical energy that was literally leaking out of him.

Ever since I was summoned to this world, I had been able to kind of see when people were using magic. It was faint, but I could make out the traces of their magic energy working their spells. I had never seen this before, though. This boy was just dumping out magical energy like it was burning a hole in his pocket. It didn't seem like he was casting a spell either as the energy would quickly dissipate. The effect resulted in something akin to an aura around him.

As Frederick and the young man approached, I became able to hear their conversation.

"Thank you again, instructor, for taking the time to answer my questions," the boy said.

"Not a problem. That's what I'm paid to do after all. Did you need anything else?" Frederick replied.

"There was one last thing. I'd like to take the upcoming practical exam early. I have some family matters that I need to attend to during the normal exam period and will be away. I promise you that I'll hold on to my top spot even without the extra time."

"Rather confident, aren't you? Well, I suppose you've earned that right. You've held the top score in your year ever since you arrived. Don't get too comfortable, though. Otherwise, you'll find yourself getting passed in no time."

"So, I have your permission then?"

"Yes. I'll arrange things with the headmistress and get back to you with a date and time. Now, if you'll excuse me, I have some other matters to attend to."

"Of course," the boy bowed, "Thank you for your time, instructor."

He then turned on his heel and headed back in the other direction. He eventually turned the corner and headed toward the courtyard, disappearing from sight. Frederick came over and opened the door without saying a word, and we entered his office. Unlike last time, he locked the door behind us.

"Forgive my lateness," he said, "as you could see, I was held up by a student."

"About that, just who is that boy? He seems...special."

"Oh, so you noticed? Well, that's not surprising, I guess. He does have a certain air about him, no?"

"I suppose you could say that. Anyway, who is he?"

"Ah, right. That is Alexander Bestroff. He's the second son of the Bestroff family, the most influential noble family in the entire alliance. He's also the number one student in your master's year by a landslide."

Lesti has to beat that kind of monster? We're going to have our work cut out for us. Hopefully, I can learn some useful information from this familiar expert of Frederick's.

I paused for a moment, surprised by my own thoughts. *Us? When did I start including myself in Lesti's problems?* Apparently, I was getting more attached to the girl than I had realized.

"My apologies," Frederick continued, "but could you wait just a few more minutes? I'd like to get some things organized before heading down."

"Sure, I don't mind," I replied.

Down? Is his friend underground then? I looked around Frederick's office for some sort of staircase. His office was smaller than most. Since it was located in one of the towers, the room took up the portion of the first floor that wasn't occupied by the staircase. There was only enough room for a simple desk and a small bookcase that sat against the back wall.

The room wasn't very decorated, but the wall on the right did bare a simple cloth banner. The banner bore a red field. The head of a black fanged beast, similar to the one on Frederick's hand, adorned the center of the banner. It looked like a banner for a military unit rather than a family crest. I turned to ask Frederick about it when I realized something.

That's odd. The tower is round, and the staircase spirals up the wall, but this room is perfectly square. That seems like an odd design choice. The room would have had much more space if they had just followed the shape of the tower.

As I pondered about the shape of the room, Frederick finished his task and walked over to the bookshelf. He placed his hand on the side and released a small amount of magical energy. The spot under his hand lit up with a green light as a small magic circle formed. A moment later, the bookcase slid effortlessly to the side, revealing a small hidden room between the wall of the room and the outer wall of the tower.

"Shall we?" Frederick asked before ducking into the newly revealed room.

I followed him through and found the room to be empty except for a ladder sticking out of a ten-foot square hole. Frederick was already starting down the ladder. He stopped, only his shoulders and head sticking out and held his hand out to me.

"It's rather far down, so I'll have to carry you."

"If you insist."

I walked over, and he scooped me up into his hand and put me on his shoulder. I extended my claws into the fabric to be extra safe as he began to descend. Frederick summoned a magical light, allowing me to see all the way to the bottom of the hole. The entire drop was about twenty feet, and the floor below was made of the same stone as the walls.

A staircase awaited us once we reached the bottom of the ladder. Rather than being straight, it followed a gentle curve. We followed it back toward the center of the school grounds. After descending for about 5 minutes, I began to feel the air grow moist. Shortly after, the staircase stopped, and we entered a much more natural-looking tunnel.

The walls were made of uncut stone, and the sound of dripping water could be heard coming from ahead. As Frederick continued down the tunnel, stalactites began to appear on the ceiling. The moisture in the air condensed on the ceiling and eventually dripped down from the stalactites, causing small pools of clear water to form under them. I would occasionally see tunnels branching off the one we were walking through.

"These caves are pretty extensive, do they spread out under the whole city?" I asked.

"That's correct. They may even extend further than that. No one has really bothered to chart the entire thing," Frederick replied, "The secret passageway we came through was built back when the school was first constructed as an emergency escape route. It was originally intended to extend outside the city, but they dug straight into this cave system by accident."

"I can see how that would put a stop to their plans. It would be incredibly difficult to dig around a cave system like this. Anyway, what is this acquaintance of yours doing all the way down here? I hope you aren't taking me to meet some shady character."

"You'll understand soon enough," Frederick said with a smirk on his face.

That's not very reassuring.

As we continued walking, I started to pick up on the faint sound of running water. It wasn't long before the tunnel opened up into a large cavern. The space was so large that Frederick's light barely covered a tenth of the whole thing. Nearby, a small stream flowed into the cave and deposited into a large pool. It was hard to tell through the darkness, but the pool appeared to be about thirty feet across. The stream continued down a tunnel on the other side.

As Frederick continued to walk along the edge of the pool, a strange sense of unease came over me. I wasn't sure why, but it felt like we were being watched. It was different from the presence I had felt watching me in the school.

My fur bristled slightly, and my ears twitched around as I searched for the source of my discomfort. I was able to pick up on the sound of breathing coming from somewhere in the cavern. I couldn't pinpoint it exactly, but I could tell that whatever the was making the sound was rather large.

"Frederick, there's something in here with us, something big," I warned.

"Ah that," Frederick said as he came to a stop by a small stone pedestal, "I'm aware. There's no need to be afraid, though. He's mostly harmless."

Frederick placed his hand on the stone pedestal and let his magical energy flow through it. A small white magic circle formed under his hand. Slowly, magical lights began to appear throughout the cavern until it was fully illuminated.

"It's beautiful," I said involuntarily.

Pale white stalactites hung from all over the high ceiling, and the lights flitted between them like wild spirits. The glow from each one danced off the water on the stalactites, making them sparkle. The still water of the pool reflected the scene above almost perfectly, giving it an otherworldly effect.

WHAT I WANT

I stared at the scene in wonder for a moment until I felt a warm puff of air on my back. Remembering the presence from earlier, I quickly turned around only to find myself face to face with a massive black dragon. My fur immediately stood on end. I dug my claws into Frederick's shoulder and let out an involuntary hiss.

"Oh, is this the one you were mentioning before, Frederick? The familiar that rambunctious red-head summoned?" the dragon asked.

"That's correct. Her name is Astria. Astria, this is Skell. He's my familiar. You know, the expert on familiars that I was telling you about? Well, now that I've introduced you, I'll be heading back."

Frederick then promptly took me off his shoulder and started back the way we had come.

"Hold on a second! You're just going to leave me here with a frickin' dragon!? What's stopping him from just eating me?"

"Eat you? Don't be silly, I'm a familiar. We don't need to eat. Besides, a tiny thing like you wouldn't be worth the effort."

Frederick continued to walk away, so I made one last desperate plea.

"Wait! You can't leave me. I won't be able to climb the ladder on my own!"

Frederick finally stopped, but when he turned around, I lost all hope. A wicked grin, unlike any I had seen before, was plastered on his face.

"Well then, you'll just have to learn enough to be able to get back on your own, won't you? Good luck."

He then turned around and continued walking back toward the tunnel. I quickly moved to run after him, but I was promptly lifted up by the scruff of my neck. My body went limp as I hung between two massive dragon claws.

Training

I smacked a small rock into the nearby cavern wall. Since Frederick had left and Skell had finally let me down, I had been venting my anger by pretending this particular rock was Frederick's face. *I can't believe that jerk just left me down here! Next time I see him, I'm going to give him a thrashing like he's never seen before.*

"How long do you intend to keep sulking?" Skell asked, "Smacking that rock around isn't going to get you out of here any faster, you know."

"Oh, shut it! I just wanted to know about familiars. I didn't ask to be trapped in a cave with a dragon. I have every right to be mad!"

Skell lowered his massive head down to eye level and glared at me.

"You must be feeling awfully bold if you're willing to tell me to shut it. Maybe I'm feeling hungry after all."

He exposed his fangs slightly and flicked his forked tongue over them. I immediately froze in the middle of taking another swing at the rock. I let out a nervous laugh and tried to compose myself. *Okay, Astria, just take deep breaths and stop insulting the dragon.*

"S-Sorry about that. I lost myself there for a moment. It's an honor to meet you, Skell, was it? My name is Astria."

"Much better," Skell replied with a satisfied nod, "Seems you have some manners after all. My name is Skell, and as I'm sure you've realized, I'm Frederick's familiar. He's asked me to instruct you on the basics of being a familiar. I'd like to get started right away if you don't mind?"

"Sure. That's what I came here for after all."

Besides, you'll just threaten me again if I say otherwise.

TRAINING

Skell raised his head back up to normal height, causing my body to relax naturally. It really was terrifying being face to face with a creature that could swallow you whole.

"Well then, where should we start?" Skell asked.

"I'm pretty much clueless, so if you could start from the beginning, that would be helpful."

"I see. That sounds rather tedious, but I suppose it was a request from Frederick. Very well, let's start with the enhancement of your natural abilities then. Those should be the easiest to understand."

"Natural abilities? What do you mean?"

"It's rather simple. Any abilities you had as an Astral Cat before you were summoned would be amplified. For example, as a dragon, my flame breath became more powerful, and my ability to store magical energy was greatly increased."

"Um, so, would you happen to know what abilities an Astral Cat like myself might have?"

"Well, yes. I happen to be familiar with the abilities of Astral Cats, but why are you ask-," Skell paused and brought his face closer to mine, narrowing his eyes, "You don't know what abilities you're supposed to have, do you?"

Oh crap, he's onto me! I need to come up with some sort of excuse.

"Y-yeah. I, um, I have amnesia!" I replied as I averted my eyes to avoid the dragon's gaze, "That's right. I can't remember a single thing since before I was summoned."

"Oh, is that so?"

"Totally, why else would I have a name like Astria. I only let Lesti call me something so simple because I can't remember my real name."

"I see. I suppose that makes sense. I was wondering why you had such a simple name."

Yes! He bought it!

"Anyway, hurry up and tell me about my abilities. I'd like to get out of this cave sometime this week."

"Right, right. I was getting to it," Skell's tail began to tap lightly on the ground, "Well, Astral Cats have two key abilities. First, they can sense the

51

flow of magical energy. Second, they can adjust their physical forms slightly to fit their environment or need."

"Oh, is that why I can see when people use spells then?"

"I've never heard of that ability, but that's most likely the case. Even familiars of the same species aren't guaranteed to have the same abilities. How each unique trait manifests will depend on the individual."

"What about that the second power you mentioned? Do I just not have that one? As far as I can tell, I can't change my shape in any way."

"That is strange, but I do believe you should have the ability," Skell stopped tapping his tail and looked at me closely, "Rather, I can tell that you absolutely do have such an ability just by looking at you."

I furrowed my brow at such a confident declaration.

"What do you mean?"

"Perhaps it would be easier to see for yourself."

Skell raised one enormous claw and pointed to the nearby pool of water. I paused for a moment and gathered myself before I began to walk over. *I wonder what I look like? I haven't seen myself since I was reborn.* My thoughts continued on as I walked over to the pool.

When I finally arrived at the water's edge, the water was blurry, and it was a bit hard to see my reflection. I sat down and waited a moment for the water to calm. When it did, I was met with the image of a cat with pale blue eyes. The form reflected in the water was small and lean. My short fur was a glossy silver color that I had never seen on an animal before. It reminded me of a shining star. Otherwise, I looked just like any other cat.

"I don't understa-."

My words were cut short by what I saw out of the corner of my vision. As I turned my head to talk to Skell, my form blurred slightly, giving it an almost ethereal appearance. When I had approached the water, I had thought that it wasn't still, and that was why I couldn't see my reflection. That wasn't the case, though. I couldn't see my reflection because I had been moving.

"W-What is this!? Why am I all blurry?"

I waved my tail around, staring wide-eyed as it left a blurry trail behind it.

"Your form isn't solid. An Astral Cat's body is a reflection of their will. It

TRAINING

will shift and bend based on what they desire, within reason anyway."

"So, you're saying that I desire to be a house cat?"

"In a sense. This appears to be your body's natural state, at the very least. Usually, Astral Cats will revert to a form that best fits their personality when they aren't consciously changing their shape. For you, this appears to be a simple house cat."

I guess I'm stuck in this form because it's the type of cat I'm most familiar with. I tore my gaze away from the water and looked back at Skell again.

"So, the fact that my body gets all blurry when I move means I should be able to change my shape, right?"

"That's right. Most Astral Cats can only change their size and body type by a relatively small amount. They wouldn't be able to go from being a house cat to a large hunter. Being a familiar though, you might be able to break past this limit."

"So, what do I need to do then? How do I become a fierce tiger?" I asked as my tail swished back and forth.

"Tiger? I'm not really sure what that is, but you just need to imagine yourself as the form you desire. If you have a strong enough will and enough magical energy, it should work."

"Alright, here I go then."

I closed my eyes and focused. I slowly but surely built up the image of a fierce tiger in my mind. Once it was complete, I imagined my body shifting and morphing like mist to become that very same tiger.

"Oh! So this is the tiger creature you spoke of? It's rather cute."

"Huh? Cute?" I replied as I opened my eyes, "What the heck!? Why am I so tiny!?"

My reflection was now a perfect mirror image of the tiger I had constructed in my mind except for one thing. I was still nearly the same size. I looked more like a cute and cuddly stuffed animal than I did a fierce predator.

"What happened? I wasn't this small in my mind, so why have I barely grown at all?"

"It's most likely that you don't possess enough magical energy to sustain the form that you desired, so you ended up as a miniature version instead."

"I thought I was supposed to be some sort of super familiar though. At least, that's the impression I got when I was talking to everyone in the headmistress's office. Shouldn't I have magical energy to spare?"

"Normally, yes. Unfortunately, I can't sense magical energy like you can, so I can't really diagnose the issue," Skell shrugged his shoulders, "For now, stay in that form. It will help you get used to maintaining a transformation."

"I have to stay like this!? I look like a child's stuffed animal!"

"It's necessary if you want to master the ability. No complaining. Now, let's move on to your other ability. I'm going to cast a spell. I want you to watch and tell me exactly what you see."

I nodded, and Skell turned to face a nearby pillar. I focused my gaze on him and waited for him to start his chant, but it never came. Without a word, magical energy started to flow out of his body and manipulate the environment around him. Tendrils of magic reached out and gathered water from the air and the nearby pool. Even more magical energy clustered around the pillar. Cold air began to radiate from the pillar, and ice started to form around it. Before long, the entire thing was encased in a thick block of ice.

"That was amazing," I ran over and inspected the pillar, "I should have expected as much from a dragon. Lesti struggles just to make an ice wall, but you encased that entire pillar like it was nothing!"

"That's probably because her instructions aren't clear enough. Did you see any differences between how our magical energies behaved?"

"Oh, yeah. I noticed that your magic was doing two different things. Part of it was gathering the water, and the other part was doing something to make it really cold, right? How did you do that?"

"You could see all that then? Fascinating," Skell closed his eyes in thought, "I don't think I've ever heard of anyone or anything being able to actually see magical energy like you can."

"Hey, answer my question! How were you able to use magic like that?"

"Ah, my apologies," He opened his eyes once more and turned to face me, "It's rather simple actually. I just provided clear instructions about what I wanted to happen. As I cast the spell, I make my intentions incredibly clear and precise. The reason your master isn't able to do the same is because she is still using basic imaging techniques, which aren't as effective as well-worded instructions."

"Wait, you can just tell magic what you want? I thought you had to have a clear image of the end result you desired. If you can do that, then why would anybody use simple images, and why is the school teaching that?"

"An excellent question!" Smoked puffed out of his nostrils at his exclamation, causing me to take a step back, "To put it rather simply, using instruction-based magic can be dangerous for beginners. Imaging provides a concrete result that the caster's magic will try and fulfill. Instructions, however, don't necessarily have a clearly defined goal."

I tilted my head to the side as I tried to take in what Skell was saying.

"Sorry, I guess I'm just having a hard time imagining a scenario where instructions would be less clear than an image."

"Very well, let's use the spell I just cast as an example. If you used imaging magic, you would picture the pillar encased in ice. Since you have a clear image, your magic would know to encase only the pillar in ice. However, if you just gave instructions like, 'Encase that pillar in ice,' then any number of things could go wrong. For instance, the wrong pillar could be encased. Imagine how catastrophic it would be if you tried to hit one of your enemies with this spell but ended up hitting your ally instead. It would probably cost them their life."

"Ah, I see what you mean. So, when using instruction-based magic, you need to give very clear and concise instructions. Otherwise, your magic may do something you don't intend it to."

"That's correct," Skell nodded approvingly, "You're a rather quick study."

That makes sense then why they wouldn't want to start children out with instruction-based magic. I can see Lesti causing all sorts of havoc with that.

"Alright, that all makes sense, but how does that relate to my ability to see magical energy?"

"Yes, let me explain. There is a form of magic used by higher-level mages and familiars called spell jamming. I believe you are particularly suited to use this type of magic."

"Spell jamming? Like preventing someone from casting a spell?"

"That's right. It's a very difficult form of magic. Most people can't even prevent basic spells. It almost requires you to read your target's mind. You have to understand how their spell works and then use your own magic to interfere with the magical energies performing that spell."

"I see how that would be difficult. You'd either need to be a mind reader or have incredibly good intuition. Even more so if your opponent isn't using an incantation."

"That's right, but you don't have any such disadvantage," Skell pointed a large claw at me, "You can see how your target's magic is working with your eyes. That means that as long as you have enough magical energy and skill, you can jam any spell."

Skell then stood up and walked about twenty feet away before turning back to face me. It was awe-inspiring to watch such a large creature moving about. Despite his size, he moved with a smoothness and agility that reminded me of a cat.

"Now then, we'll begin practicing right away. I'm going to try and hit you with a simple water spell, and I want you to jam it. Let's begin."

"Wait. I don't know how to-."

My protest was immediately cut short as I was doused with a ball of ice-cold water that had appeared above my head. I stood there, fur dripping wet, glaring at Skell for a moment before shaking the excess water off.

"I told you to wait! I don't know how to control my magical energy at all!"

I dodged to the side as a second ball of water came crashing down where I was standing once again.

"I already told you everything you need to know about magical theory. You just have to apply it."

Skell continued to try and douse me in water as I dodged around in a panic. *I barely even have time to dodge much less work on a counter. How is this supposed to be training!?* The image of Frederick's smile as he left the cave passed through my mind. *Those two are totally meant for each other.*

"Whoa!"

I barely escaped two balls of water that came at me from either side by jumping backward. *I need to do something. I can't focus on jamming his magic like this. I need to move faster.*

As that thought passed through my mind, I felt a small pulse of magic ripple through my body. I jumped to avoid the next ball of water and flew ten feet into the air. My magical energy had responded to my instructions and provided a boost to my body. Unfortunately, this also left me completely exposed. Another water sphere slammed into my face, drenching me completely.

Well, that wasn't what I wanted. I need to be more specific. Of course, Skell wasn't going to give me a chance to get my thoughts in order. Another projectile was on its way by the time my feet hit the ground.

"You jerk! At least give me a chance to dry off!" I shouted at Skell as I continued to dodge.

"If you have time to talk, then you should have plenty of time to dry yourself off with magic."

Three water balls formed around me and began circling me. They move slightly closer with each rotation, leaving me no room to escape. *Alright, it's now or never. I really hope this works!* I then focused on the source of the magic I had felt within myself before and issued a command. *Continuously reinforce my body with enough magical energy that I can move up to twice as fast as normal.*

I immediately felt magic pulse through my body, but it didn't fade this time. Instead, it continuously flowed through me. I crouched down and leapt over the wall of water just before it collapsed on me. As soon as I escaped into the air, another ball was flying towards me. However, I was ready this time.

I once again reached into my magic pool and issued a command. *Send the incoming water sphere back at Skell!* Without missing a beat, a tendril of magic lashed out and smacked the sphere of water directly back at Skell. Unfortunately, he just swiped the projectile away casually with his massive claws, and the shot never landed. Still, I had managed to counter his spell somewhat.

I landed on my feet in a ready position, expecting another wave of attacks to come my way. However, Skell just stared at me with a thoughtful expression on his face instead.

"What's wrong? Had enough already?" I asked.

"No, no. I'm just surprised," he replied, "I've trained countless wyrmlings and even a fair number of humans in my time, but I've never seen anyone pick up on my teachings quite so quickly."

"Really? It doesn't seem that hard. All I did was use magic to constantly reinforce my body."

"Astria, what wording did you use for that spell?" Skell asked in a slightly panicked sounding voice, "Actually, never mind that. Cancel whatever spell you cast this instant!"

"Huh? O-Okay."

I inadvertently took a step backward because of his intensity. He seemed worried about something, though, so I quickly issued a command to cancel the reinforcement spell. *Stop reinforcing my body with magical energy.* I immediately felt the flow of magic in my body begin to slow and come to a stop.

"Okay. It's do-."

Suddenly, the world blurred in front of me. My body felt like it weighed ten times its normal weight, and I could barely stand. I slowly crumpled to the ground as I fought to stay conscious. Darkness crawled into the corners of my vision, and my world faded to black.

* * *

When I next opened my eyes, I was lying curled up next to Skell's massive frame. The heat from his body was in stark contrast to the cool, moist air of the cavern. The two blended together to form a comforting sensation. It reminded me of sitting next to a heater with a blanket on a cold, rainy day. Now, all I needed was a book.

"Ow. My head."

Unfortunately, I couldn't enjoy my situation in the least. I had the worst headache of my life. It felt like someone had hit me over the head with a baseball bat. I squeezed my eyes closed to try and stem the pain. It helped a little, but I was still in enough pain that I let out a mental groan.

"Oh, you're awake?" Skell asked.

"Yeah. Though I almost wish I wasn't. My head feels like it was stepped on by a dragon."

Skell's brought his head around to look me over with a chuckle.

"You're lucky to have a headache at all. If you hadn't canceled the spell when you did, you would have died. You ran out of magical energy and passed out. Normally, your magic would recover over time, resulting in the symptoms you're experiencing now. However, since you didn't put any sort of termination clause in your spell, it would have continued to drain you magic for all time. You would never have regained enough energy to wake up."

"Seriously? Don't you think you should have warned me about that before we started?"

I smacked Skell in the side as my tail twitched back and forth in irritation.

"My apologies," he replied, lowering his head in what seemed like a bow, "I didn't think you would pick up on my teachings so quickly. My oversight put you in danger. I've failed you as an instructor."

"Well, it turned out alright in the end. I learned how dangerous the misuse of instruction-based magic is, and I'm not dead," I lowered my head in return, "Thanks for warning me, Skell. I would have died for sure if you hadn't told me to cancel the spell."

"I'm only glad that I managed to warn you in time. It would have been quite the blunder to lose my new student on the first day." Skell said as he stood up and walked over to the pool, "That being said, whenever you have recovered sufficiently, we should continue your training. We've already lost a lot of time due to this mishap."

"Wait, how long was I out for?"

Skell picked up a decent-sized rock and used magic to reshape it into a crude bowl, which he filled with water from the pool.

"You suffered severe magic depletion, so it took you longer to recover than usual. You've been sleeping for almost an entire day."

Skell walked back over and placed the now full bowl down next to me.

"Drink some water if you can. I'll find you something to eat in the meantime."

"I thought you said that familiars didn't need to eat?"

"I'm surprised you remember. That's correct. As familiars, we don't need to eat and drink. However, it does help us to recover our magical energy faster."

"I see. It'll be hard with my head pounding like this, but I'll do my best to eat. I should try and get back as soon as possible. Lesti is probably worried sick."

"Oh, if it's your master that you're worried about, don't be. Frederick should have told her where you are."

"That's a relief. Still, I'd rather not be away too long. That girl will overwork herself if I'm not around."

"Birds of a feather, eh?" Skell replied in a smug voice.

"What are you talking about? I'm nothing like that."

"Oh, no. Of course not. Anyway, I'm off to find you a tasty snack."

"Alright, I guess."

With that, Skell turned and walked deeper into the caves. *I wonder what he meant about Lesti and I being birds of a feather? I know I just collapsed, but that was an accident. It's totally different!*

* * *

A while later, the cavern was filled with the sounds of uncontrollable dragon laughter. Skell had returned carrying a rather large lizard he had killed. Of course, he returned at a rather embarrassing time for me. I was standing over the water bowl, and my entire face was drenched. Water dripped off my fur onto the cave floor. I probably looked as ridiculous as I felt.

"Shut up! It's not that funny!" I yelled.

"I'm sorry," Skell said between ragged breaths, "It's just, the way you were drinking water was so absurd. I couldn't help myself."

"I didn't have any other choice! I tried using my tongue, but I was barely getting any water that way!"

"Still, to dunk your entire face into the water like that. Bahahaha!"

Skell erupted into another fit of laughter. Finally, I lost my patience and sent the water bowl flying at Skell. He did his best to control himself after that, but a chuckle would occasionally slip through, earning him a nasty glare.

I felt much better after eating the lizard that he cooked. I was a little worried about how it would taste, but it surprisingly tasted like chicken. Now that I was feeling better, I was rearing to get started again.

"Alright, I'm ready now," I said as I looked up at Skell expectantly, "What are we doing this time? Are you going to throw more water balls at me?"

Skell looked at me thoughtfully for a minute, tapping his tail against the ground. *I wonder if he's worried about me messing up another spell? I almost died, after all.* I tilted my head to the side and shut my eyes tightly as I attempted to think of a way to put him at ease.

"Ah, I've got it!" My eyes snapped open, and I stood up, "I'll just call out the exact instructions I'm using for my spells. That way, you can tell me if I have any major gaps in my logic."

"Oh, that's not a bad idea," Skell stopped tapping his tail and lowered his head down to eye level with me, "Well then, why don't we give it a try before we start. Try adjusting your body augmentation spell from before so that it's safe."

"Alright, let's see," I glanced up at the lights flitting about as I tried to recall the exact wording I had used before. Once I had recalled it, I added an extra clause onto the end to prevent overuse of magic and recited my new spell aloud, "Continuously reinforce my body with enough magical energy that I can move up to twice as fast as normal. Once my magical energy stores fall to ten percent, stop reinforcing my body and end the spell."

"Not good enough," Skell replied as he slammed his tail into the ground, "Ten percent is far too vague, you need to be very specific when crafting spells like this one."

We continued to tweak the spell for a few minutes, making sure it was safe and adding in an extra feature that allowed me to adjust the output on the fly. The final wording ended up like this.

"If this spell is already active, update the active value to the given value. Otherwise, continuously reinforce my body with enough magic that I can move my normal speed multiplied by the given value. Once my magical energy stores fall to ten percent of my maximum amount of magical energy, end all effects of this spell immediately."

That's too damn long! Am I supposed to say that every time!? I'll die of old age before I can finish casting this spell.

"This isn't going to work, Skell. Isn't there any way to make these instructions shorter?"

"Of course, there is. Magic would be useless in combat if you had to recite such a long set of instructions every time. The solution is to name your spell."

"Huh? Name it?" I tilted my head to the side, "How does that help?"

"Well, think about it. Why do we give names to anything?"

"Isn't that so that we can talk about them?"

"No, no. That's far too simple," Skell replied as he shook his head, "For example, you could talk about a dragon by calling it a giant scaled monster with wings and claws that breathes fire, but that's very inefficient. Instead, you call it a dragon. Naming things allows us to convey large amounts of information quickly."

"Oh! I get it, but doesn't that only work if both parties use the same name for something? How does magical energy even know names?"

"That's a question that even I don't have the answer to, but it is possible. You can train your own magical energy to associate certain words or phrases with a spell. For example," Skell stood up and faced the pool of water, "Aqua Sphere."

A sphere of water like the ones he had used during our training session earlier appeared above the pool. It slowly floated up until it hit the stalactites on the ceiling and popped, sending water raining down on the pool. I watched in amazement as each step of the spell formed in the air around him. It was rather complex as it required water to be gathered, held together in a sphere, and then propelled toward a target.

"As you can see, a name makes casting even moderately difficult spells rather simple. Make sure you give your spells a unique name though, something you don't normally use in everyday speech. The spell will activate no matter what context you use its name in."

"Alright," I sat and stared at the water for a moment in thought, my tail swishing back and forth, "I think I'll call my spell Speed Boost. So, what do I need to do to build up an association between the instructions for my spell and its name?"

Skell's eyes became filled with a wicked look as he turned to face me, letting me know that I was in for something awful.

"The key is repetition. Starting now, you're going to activate your spell three hundred times and say its name afterward each time."

"Y-you're kidding, right?"

Skell slammed his tail on the ground again, causing me to jump.

"I don't joke when it comes to learning magic. Now, get started. I'm going to go find us some more food so we can recharge our magic."

"Alright, alright. I'll do it."

I let out a heavy sigh and began my torturous task.

Magic Circles

A hail of stones smashed into the ground where I was standing as I leapt into the air to dodge. I was almost immediately met with a ball of fire. I had been expecting this, though. After a whole week of training, I had learned that it was one of Skell's favorite tactics.

"Air Walk!" I called out the name of a spell. Air Walk was a bit of a misnomer as you weren't actually walking on air. Instead, it created a platform by solidifying magical energy. You could then stand on or jump off this platform, making it look like you were walking on air.

I jumped off a series of platforms, dodging back and forth as Skell continued to hurl fireballs at me. The heat from his spells was starting to cause a small amount of steam to build up in the cavern, making it harder to see. I decided to use this to my advantage, ducking under a fireball and lunging forward through the haze to try and close the distance.

Unfortunately, the low visibility worked against me in this case, and I leapt straight into another fireball. I quickly cast another spell in a panic. "Energy Barrier!" Energy Barrier was a spell that created a barrier directly in front of me that would redirect projectiles to the side. I breathed a quick sigh of relief as soon as the fireball was safely shoved aside and shut off the spell. It used a large amount of magical energy, so it was best not to leave it on for too long.

I burst out of the cloud of steam and landed on the ground directly in front of Skell, who was reared up on his hind legs. His head nearly touched the ceiling when he stood up like that. Half a dozen fireballs and another dozen floating stones hovered in the air around him. I charged forward before he could send them all crashing down on my head.

Almost immediately, a stone came crashing down in my path. I quickly sidestepped it and used Energy Barrier to divert the fireballs that were coming my direction. I continued moving forward like this, dodging the stones to save energy and diverting the fireballs. Skell must have caught onto what I was doing because several large stones came crashing down in front of me, all at once, forming a wall.

Before I could even react, fireballs came at me from all directions. "Speed Boost Times Three!" I boosted my speed by three times and leapt towards Skell's head using an energy barrier to deflect the one fireball in my path. With my extra speed, I was on top of him before he could react. He tried to swat me out of the air with one of his claws, but I quickly used Air Walk to somersault over it.

My trajectory put me directly above the massive dragon's head. *I've finally got you, you giant jerk!* I glared down at him and cast one last spell. "Power Cat Times Ten!" I felt a massive surge of magic pulse through my body. Pushing off the ceiling above, I rocketed towards my target. "Take this!" I did a quick twist in the air to build up extra momentum and swung my paw straight down on Skell's head.

My paw stopped centimeters from its target as it collided with a powerful barrier of magical energy. Not willing to give up yet, I pushed off of it to gain some distance. Then, I used Air Walk to propel myself toward my target once again, smashing into the barrier. This time the force from my strike broke through it, leaving my target vulnerable.

"Hahaha! Take this, you overgrown lizard! This is payback for my tail!" With my victory at hand, I could no longer control my anger and lashed out at Skell verbally. I swung my paw down with all my might onto the top of his head with my claws extended. Even at ten times my normal strength, I knew it wouldn't kill him. It would give him a nasty headache, though. It might even break some of his scales.

Tink!

"Huh?" I stared at where my claws had collided with Skell's head. Not only had I not broken his scales, there wasn't even a scratch on him. After a moment, I noticed that both my Speed Boost and Power Cat spells had stopped functioning. I had run out of magical energy at the crucial moment.

Oh, shit. Remembering the insult that I had hurled at Skell just moments before, I began to panic. If I were still human, I would have broken out in a cold sweat. Instead, I folded my ears back against my head and sat perfectly still, hoping he would forget that I existed.

If there was one thing I had learned about the massive black dragon, it was that combat and training brought out his wicked side. He didn't know the meaning of holding back or mercy. The burnt end of my tail was a testament to that. Over the last week, I had been pummeled by rocks, doused with freezing water, and scorched with balls of fire. It was never enough to cause any serious injuries, but it still hurt.

I was plucked off the dragon's head by the scruff of my neck and soon found myself face to face with him. *I'm dead. This is it. He's going to kill me.*

"That was a rather bold declaration you made just now," he narrowed his eyes at me and let a puff of smoke out of his nostrils.

"Y-Yeah. Sorry about that. I just got a little hot-headed, you know?"

"Well, then maybe you should take a minute to cool off."

With that, Skell unceremoniously tossed me into the nearby pool of water.

* * *

After hauling my exhausted body out of the water and shaking myself off, I plopped down on my side like a dead fish. Before long, the scent of cooked meat began to waft through the cavern. *Smells like giant lizard again.* Skell had been preparing cooked meat after each of our training sessions to help me recover. While he would eat too, I doubted he needed the energy as much as I did. He seemed to have an inexhaustible supply of magical energy. Once the meat was finished cooking, I got up and walked over to join him.

"How was your swim? Cool off a little?" he asked as he laid a piece of cooked lizard haunch down in front of me.

"I'll be lucky if I don't catch a cold."

I glared at him for a moment before tearing into the meat. It had taken me awhile to get used to eating without hands. At first, I had tried really hard to avoid getting anything on my face, but that made the whole process too slow. So, I gave up on that and just cleaned myself up afterwards. After I had eaten my fill, I sat back and talked to Skell while I groomed myself.

"Still, I almost had you this time," I watched him out of the corner of my eye to see his reaction, "If I hadn't run out of magical energy I would have finally landed a decent blow."

"You certainly have improved," he chomped down on the cooked head of the lizard and looked me square in the eye, "But you've still got a long way to go before you can beat me."

Much as I hate to admit it, he's probably right. My magical energy runs out way too fast. The amount of magical energy I could use had slowly been getting better, but it was still a far cry from Skell's seemingly bottomless pool. I still couldn't take on the form of any large cats. A bobcat was about the best that I could manage at this point.

I finished my grooming and plopped back down on my side.

"Why do you have so much magical energy anyway?"

"Dragons are born with large pools of magical energy. It's necessary for us to be able to fly. Our wings alone wouldn't be able to hold us up, so we use magic to help keep us in the air. Becoming Frederick's familiar then further multiplied my pool of magical energy."

"Lucky. I wish I had even a portion of your magical energy." I rolled over on my back and stared up at the ceiling.

"I do find it strange that your magic pool is so small. Considering your level of intelligence, I would have expected you to have a much higher limit."

"Oh, well. There's no point fretting over it, I suppose, " I rolled back over and stood up, "I'll just have to continue training once I go back up to the school."

"Quite true. Speaking of which, I think it's about time that you return. I've taught you everything that I can for now, and Frederick tells me that your master is getting rather insistent about meeting you."

"Lesti has?" My ears perked up at the mention of the girl who had summoned me to this world.

"She's been bothering him multiple times a day for the last few days apparently," Skell said as he licked the grease from the lizard meat off of his claws, "He says that if she bothers him one more time that he might just throw her down in the caves to shut her up."

I can actually see him doing that. I should head back before she ends up lost down here. I'll have to thank Frederick for putting up with her too. Hey, wait a second...

"Skell, when did you talk to Frederick?" I started prowling towards the dragon, "I haven't seen him down here all week."

"Oh, we were communicating telepathically," he said without even bothering to look at me, "Familiars and their masters can communicate up to a mile apart."

I lunged at Skell and attempted to swat him on the head, but I was intercepted mid-jump by his lightning-fast claws.

"Why didn't you tell me that at the beginning!?" I squirmed and flailed at Skell to no avail, "I could have kept in touch with her this whole time!"

"Honestly, it just slipped my mind. You already knew how to communicate privately, so I just assumed you had figured out the effective range by now. Anyway, rather than try to hit me, why don't you give it a try."

I groaned, trying to shove my annoyance at Skell down so I could focus on what was important. Slowly, I drew a deep breath. "Lesti?" I called out, closing my eyes and focusing on the image of the red-headed girl in my mind, "Lesti, can you hear me?"

"Astria!?" Lesti's panicked voice rang through my head, "Where are you? Are you okay?"

"Relax, I'm fine. I'm getting ready to head back."

"Don't tell me to relax! I haven't heard from you in a week! I was worried that Frederick had done something awful to you."

I felt a sense of guilt wash over me. She sounded like she was on the verge of tears. At the same time, I was happy. *When was the last time someone was this worried about me?* A gentle warm feeling began to spread through my chest.

"Thanks for worrying about me, Lesti. I promise I'm okay, though."

"Of course I worried about you!" her voice had relaxed a little, "We're partners, aren't we?"

"I guess you're right," I said with a chuckle, "Anyway, where are you?"

"I'm in class right now."

"Okay. Stay there. I'll come find you."

"Alright, but you had better explain where you've been when you get back."

"I will. I promise. Alright, I've got to go. See you soon."

I broke the connection and opened my eyes to find that I was no longer hanging in the air. I had been so focused that I hadn't noticed that Skell had put me down.

"You seem rather pleased," he said.

"It's a nice feeling, having someone worry about you."

"I suppose it is," Skell gazed off into the cave for a moment before continuing, "I imagine you'll be going then?"

"Yeah. I've got to go and make sure that girl isn't running herself ragged," I stared up at my mentor's face far above, "I promise I'll come to visit you though. It has to be boring spending all your time down in this cave with only Frederick to keep you company after all."

"I would like that," Skell lowered his head so that he was eye level with me, "Be careful out there, Astria. Humans can be greedy creatures. There are those who will covet your power if they learn of it."

"I know. I'll be careful."

I turned and faced off toward the tunnel that I had come in just a week before, but then I hesitated for just a moment. There was something that I had been wanting to ask Skell all week, but I was scared. I wasn't sure whether it was because I was afraid he would find out I used to be human or I just didn't want to hear the truth. Either way, I was out of time. It was now or never.

"Hey, Skell?" I called out looking back over my shoulder, "Do you think it would be possible to use my transformation abilities to transform into something other than a cat?"

"Hmm. What exactly do you mean?" He looked at me with a puzzled expression on his face.

"For example, could I turn into a dog, a dragon, or," I hesitated for a moment, second guessing myself before deciding to push through, "or even a human?

I mean, with enough practice, of course."

Skell looked at me for a long moment before responding, "I can only guess based on what I've seen before, but it seems unlikely. Astral Cats project their form into this world based on their soul. It's already incredible that you can change your form as much as you can."

"I see," I felt my heart sink a little at his response. *I guess I'm going to be stuck like this forever then.* I looked up at the ceiling for a minute and steeled my resolve, remembering Lesti's words. *This new life is my chance to start over. Even if I can't become human again, I'm sure I can live happily.*

"I'll be going then," I looked back at Skell one last time, "See you soon."

With that, I took off down the tunnel.

* * *

After leaving Skell, I used Speed Boost to quickly make my way back to the ladder that Frederick and I had climbed down. Once there, I used Air Walk to make my way back up the shaft and Power Cat to pull the bookcase out of my way.

The door to Frederick's office was slightly ajar. Luckily, it was unlikely that anyone had seen me since I had only moved the bookcase enough to squeeze by. After making sure to push the bookcase back into place, I made my way out into the hall.

I squinted to avoid being blinded as the sun's light shone on my face for the first time in a week. I made my way down the mostly empty hallways until I was outside of Lesti's classroom. I could hear Lani giving a lecture inside and considered waiting until the class was over so as not to interrupt. Lesti would definitely make a scene after all.

I decided against waiting since there was a good chance she would make a scene anyway if I didn't show up after I had promised her I would. I took a deep breath and walked into the classroom. I tried to act casual so as to avoid drawing too much attention and interrupting the lesson.

"Astria!"

My plan was foiled as Lesti leapt up from her seat with a shout as soon as I entered the room. Before I could even react, she had dashed over and scooped me up in a quick embrace. I was going to scold her for being rude to Lani until I noticed that she was trembling slightly.

She must have been even more worried than I realized. I rubbed my cheek against hers in an attempt to calm her nerves. It would have been a rather sweet moment if it hadn't been interrupted by a haughty voice from the back of the classroom.

"Well, would you look at that. The mangy cat has returned to her failure of a master." I looked up to see Sebastian looking down from his seat with a sneer on his face, "I thought for sure that she had abandoned you after your pathetic display of magic the other day."

"Shut your mouth, Sebastian!" Lesti stopped trembling and sent a fierce glare his way, "Astria would never abandon me for such a petty reason. She's not like you."

I'm not sure what I did to earn that kind of trust, but let him have it, girl! The room fell silent at her words, and even Lani looked slightly panicked. She tried to intervene but couldn't find a way to butt into the conversation that followed.

"And what's that supposed to mean?" Sebastian stood up at his desk, "Are you trying to say something about my character? You? The worst student in our class?"

"I don't have to be good at magic to tell what kind of person you are," Lesti sat me on the floor and turned to face Sebastian as she stood, "Everyone can tell that you're a small and petty excuse for a man. Actually, sorry, that's not quite right. You're more of a child than a man after all."

The entire classroom froze. Everyone was looking at Sebastian nervously to see how he would react. I expected him to lose his cool, but he continued to stand there with a smug look on his face.

This kid is dangerous. That thought passed through my mind briefly as I looked at him. A normal kid his age wouldn't be able to maintain his cool after being insulted like that. Normally, that would be an asset for a person, but his clear disdain for people he considered beneath him meant that asset would most likely be put to use in dangerous ways.

"So, you think I'm petty, do you?" Sebastian started walking down the stairs toward us, "That's just not true. In fact, I'll prove it to you," his gaze fixed on me, "How about making me your new master instead of this failure?"

Both Lesti and I stood in shocked silence for a moment. *How does that make you less petty exactly?* Sebastian came to a stop just in front of us and looked down at me.

"Well? What do you think?" he extended his hands out to the side as if he was trying to show me how amazing he was, "If you join me, I can make even you into one of the most famous familiars in the entire alliance. After all, I'm far more skilled than your current master."

Next to me, I could see that Lesti was getting visibly angry. Her fists were clenched at her sides, but she was still under control otherwise.

"Besides, I can offer you a much nicer life than she ever could. My family is far wealthier than hers. You'd never want for anything. So, what do you say?" he asked as he crouched down and held his hand out to me.

Like anyone would want to work for you. I smacked his hand aside with my paw and hissed at him. The smugness disappeared from his face, replaced by a dark, foreboding glare. He stood up and made to leave the classroom.

"You'll regret turning me down, mangy cat."

Sebastian walked out of the room, and the tension that was in the air finally dissipated. Lani managed to get the class focused again and continued their lesson. Since my crash course in instruction-based magic, I had no interest in these basic lessons. I tried to take a nap instead, but I was on edge from our spat with Sebastian.

No matter how much I thought about it, it didn't make sense. Why would he invite me to join him after he bad-mouthed me so much? I spent the rest of the class period pondering that question and trying to avoid the ominous feeling in the back of my mind.

* * *

Later that night, Lesti and I were in the classroom practicing her spells by candlelight. Sebastian never returned to the classroom after the incident.

Lesti was once again practicing the Ice Wall spell and failing miserably as usual. I was honestly impressed. Most people would have given up by this point, but she stuck with it the whole time I was training with Skell.

During her breaks, we filled each other in on what had happened in our time apart. Apparently, Sebastian had been harassing her every day, saying I had run away to find a new master or died. He really seemed to enjoy tormenting Lesti for some reason. That was probably his motive for inviting me to join him as well.

I left out a few details about my time in the caves. I didn't like hiding things from Lesti after seeing how worried she had been about me, but I felt it was for the best.

First, I intentionally didn't mention that Skell was a dragon. I was pretty sure it was a secret that a dragon was hiding beneath the school. That and I got the feeling that if I told her she wouldn't leave me alone until I introduced her. Second, I didn't tell her about instruction-based magic. It was dangerous, and she would definitely try and use it even if I warned her not to.

"Ah! Why can't I get this right!?" Lesti threw herself down in front of the desk that I was laying on.

Another failed attempt at an ice wall sat in the middle of the classroom. It was closer to a full wall now, but it was too thin still and was melting just as quickly as before. Now that I knew more about how magic worked; I could see the problem. Her image was lacking some really important information.

First, it didn't specify the amount of water that should be gathered and where it should come from. Secondly, it didn't have any instructions to reduce the temperature around the ice. Those two factors were why the wall was never the right shape and melted so quickly.

It was understandable though, creating a proper image for that sort of thing was difficult. It reminded me a bit of cooking recipes you could find on the internet in my old world. They would list out the instructions step by step and include pictures or videos of what you needed to do.

"At this rate, they won't let me move up to instruction-based magic," Lesti let out a heavy sigh.

"Wait, you know about instruction-based magic?" I jumped down off the desk and turned to face Lesti, "I thought they didn't teach that to students."

"Huh? Of course, I know about it," she sat upright, "It's like the worst kept secret in the entire academy. In your final year, if you do well enough on your practical exams and get permission from your instructor, you can join a special class on the subject."

"I see. I thought for sure that, if you learned about it, you would run off and try and use it yourself."

"Oh, so you think I'm that reckless, huh?" she mock glared at me before laughing loudly, "Well, you aren't wrong. I would definitely have done that if there weren't so many stories of students who tried just that dying in horrible ways," her expression took on a serious note as she continued, "I talked to Lani about it, and she warned me about just how dangerous it could be. I decided I would only use that as a last resort."

Lesti picked me up and held me just in front of her face.

"So, my dear Astria, how is it that you know about instruction-based magic? I'm pretty sure I never told you about it," she asked as she fixed me with a piercing glare.

I quickly explained how I had learned from my training sessions with Skell. At her insistence, I even went so far as to explain what I found to be difficult about the practice, which was mainly the complex instructions that were required.

"It really is a pain that there's no simple way to codify magic instructions," I complained as I finished up my story.

"Aren't you just referring to magic circles?" Lesti sat me down in her lap, "They're basically just magical instructions recorded in a special script."

"Oh, yeah. I guess that makes sense. Wait, if that's the case, then why don't more people use them? I've hardly seen any magic circles since I got here. In fact, the only person I've really seen use them is Frederick."

"In most cases, they're considered useless," Lesti began counting on her fingers, "The script is complex and hard to learn, they require a user to provide them with magic in order to function and drawing them takes forever. It took me several months to finish the summoning circle."

Lesti's explanation made sense. Magic circles lost a lot of their usefulness since they required someone to provide them with magic. That was especially true considering how difficult it was to draw them out. Still, there was something nagging at the back of my mind.

"Why do you need to draw magic circles at all?"

She shrugged, "What's the point of a magic circle if you don't draw it, right?"

I frowned and shook my head, "It's just that if magic circles are just a way of codifying magical instructions, couldn't you just imagine the magic circle in your mind like an instruction sheet? Then you'd just be able to instruct your magic to perform the steps listed out by the magic circle, right?"

Lesti stared at me with wide eyes for a moment, her mouth opening and closing silently as she tried to find some response. Then, she suddenly stood up and rushed over to the board, forcing me to bail out of her lap. She began frantically drawing a magical circle on the board. After a few minutes, it was complete.

"Alright, this magic circle should have the same effect as the magical light spell that the teachers use all the time," she said as she turned to face me, "If what you're saying actually works, then I should be able to cast that spell with perfect accuracy even though I've never practiced it before."

"Wait, wait, wait." I jumped up on the teacher's podium slightly panicked. "Are you sure you even drew that correctly? How do you even know how to write that in the first place?"

"I learned everything there is to know about magic circles when I was working on the summoning ritual. I have the instructions right here."

Before I could stop her, Lesti placed her hand on the magic circle and added a small amount of magic energy. A small orb of light appeared above her shoulder. I breathed a sigh of relief as I realized that she really had gotten the instructions right. She took her hand off the circle, causing the orb of light to disappear.

"Alright, now for the real test," she turned to face me once again, "I'm going to try casting that same spell by picturing the magic circle I just drew in my mind."

"Be careful," I pleaded as my tail twitched nervously, "If anything feels wrong or I say to stop, cancel the spell immediately, alright?"

She nodded at me without a word and closed her eyes. Several seconds passed without anything happening. *Maybe I was wrong?* Then, she slowly opened her eyes. At the same time, a glowing orb of light began to form in the space between us. We both stared at the simple light without saying a word. It worked.

Growth and Relationships

"N-now, everyone pay attention, please. I'd like to get started so that we have a chance to get through everyone."

Lani desperately tried to focus the class. Today, they would be practicing for the practical exams that were fast approaching. That meant that there wouldn't be any lectures. Instead, they would be practicing their spells on the training grounds.

The combination of being outside and getting to practice using their spells meant that the students were full of energy. That, of course, included Lesti. I had given her permission to use the new technique we had been practicing for the last week, so she was eager to get the show underway.

"A-alright, for today's practice, I'd like to see everyone use the Fireball spell," Lani finally got the class under control, "We'll be going three at a time. Would anyone like to volunteer to go first?"

"I'd like to go first!" Lesti's hand shot up like a firework.

"O-okay. That's one person. Who else?"

A nervous look appeared on Lani's face. It was understandable. Every time Lesti was involved, trouble seemed to follow shortly after. However, there was no way she could refuse when she was volunteering so eagerly.

After that, another handful of students volunteered. Lani picked two students that were somewhere in the middle of the pack in terms of skill. *I wonder if she did that to try and keep Lesti from embarrassing herself. Well, unfortunately, that's just going to make the difference even more startling.*

Lesti and the two other students took their places. Across the training ground, three sturdy looking wooden dummies had been placed in the ground. Other than those dummies, the training ground was just an empty field. Any trees were a safe distance away in order to avoid collateral damage.

Lesti stood across from the dummy on the far left while the other students took the center and right dummies, respectively. They were each about thirty feet from their target. Lani moved to a position closer to the dummies and motioned for the students to begin.

At her signal, each of the students began their chants for Fireball, and I began to see the magic take shape around the other two students. However, there wasn't any activity around Lesti. No magic coiled around her, nor did any fire begin to form.

Lani looked on with a worried expression on her face as the incantations neared their end. The girl on the right finished her incantation first. A moderately sized fireball formed in front of her. "Fireball!" At her shout, the spell raced forward. However, her aim was slightly off, and the ball of flame clipped the side of the target before dissipating.

The boy in the middle was the next to finish. Unlike the girl, his fireball moved at a far slower speed. The ball of fire hit the target square on. However, it wasn't hot enough to do anything more than scorch the surface of the hard, wooden dummy.

Lesti was the last one to finish her incantation. "Fireball!" Instantly, a large ball of flame roared to life in front of her. Its heat was intense enough that we could feel it from where we were standing. As soon as it appeared, it shot forward with enough speed to cause a powerful gust of wind. It slammed into the target, causing a small explosion at the point of impact.

As the dust settled, everyone stared dumbfounded at the aftermath of Lesti's spell. The target dummy was charred black. Both it and the dry yellow grass around it continued to burn in a few places. The one responsible stood there with her hand still extended, a look of shock on even her own face. *So much for our agreement to hold back.*

One look at Lani's face told me that our entire act had been for naught. Lesti's chant had been bluff that was meant to disguise the fact that she was using instruction-based magic. *There's no way she wouldn't figure it out after a display like that.*

Lani's gaze continuously switched back and forth between staring at the wrecked dummy and Lesti. Each time it did, her expression would morph between one of pure shock and a mixture of anger and nervousness. I was worried she was going to hurt her neck like that, so I decided to intervene.

"Shouldn't you put out those fires before they spread?"

I groomed some of the dirt and dust out of my fur as I reached out to her privately. She visibly jumped at my sudden interruption and started to put out the fires with a water spell. Once she was finished, she turned to face Lesti with trembling shoulders.

"L-Lest-. Er. No, I mean, Ms. Vilia. P-Please, come to my office immediately after class."

"Huh, why!? I did really well this time, right!?" Lesti pointed to the charred remains of the practice dummy.

"Ms. Vilia," Lani's gaze rose to meet ours, and a calm smile covered her face, "I believe I said to come to my office after class. Do you understand?"

Lani suddenly started acting like a completely different person. Her smile was calm and on the surface, but the cold aura she was putting off betrayed her inner anger and made the cool autumn air feel more like a frigid winter night. To be honest, it was freaking me out, and I wasn't the only one.

Lesti sensed the change too, and snapped to attention with a squeak, the color drained from her face, "Yes, Ma'am!"

"Excellent. Now, let's keep things moving, everyone."

Lani returned to her lesson, explaining what each of the other students had done wrong. She had stopped stuttering and still had the same terrifying smile on her face the whole time. For the students' part, they all followed instructions like well-trained soldiers. Apparently, no one wanted to step on the land mine that was Lani in her current state. Lesti returned to sit by me, the light gone from her eyes, and her face pale.

"Well, Astria, it was nice knowing you," she whispered, "I hope you have a wonderful life."

"Oh, come on. It can't be that bad. This is Lani we're talking about, right?" I looked over to find Lani staring daggers at me.

"Ms. Vilia. Please be sure to bring Astria with you to my office after class."

It felt like my blood had frozen at hearing her ice-cold voice. She sounded completely different from her normal self to the point where one might wonder if she were possessed. Apparently, our situation was far more precarious than I had thought.

***

"How could you do something so reckless!?"

Lani paced back and forth in her office while Lesti and I stood at attention. The red-orange glow from the late afternoon sun tinted the room to match Lani's mood. There was clear anger in her eyes, and her cold restraint from earlier was gone entirely, replaced by a fiery rage.

Like I had thought, Lani had immediately realized from Lesti's spell that she had used instruction-based magic. It would have been practically impossible to get that type of result otherwise. From the speed at which the fireball had formed, to the size and force of it, none of that was possible with simple imaging techniques.

I guess this is partially my fault. I told Lesti to hold back, but we never really practiced that spell beforehand, and changing the spell on the fly would have been dangerous.

"Are you even listening to me!?" Lani's shout snapped me back to reality, where I found her glaring daggers at me, "How could you let Lesti use instruction-based magic? Do you even understand how dangerous it is without proper instruction? If one thing had been off, the entire spell could have backfired, and she could have been severely injured!"

"W-well, we practiced all week, so I figured it would be fine."

I struggled to come up with a good excuse. Lesti and I had agreed to hide our discovery about magic circles from others for now. The ability to quickly and efficiently learn spells by memorizing magic circles had a ton of potential implications for this world.

Instruction-based magic was incredibly complex and abstract, which made it hard to teach and learn. Even when someone did learn how to use it, a single slip up could end their life. This made creating complex spells difficult, dangerous, and time-consuming. Combine that with a limited pool of people who could create them, and it was understandable that they were practically non-existent.

"You think a single week is enough time to practice before trying out a dangerous spell like Fireball!" Lani glared down at me angrily, "Most students spend months under the careful instruction of an expert before they even attempt their first instruction-based spell, and they certainly don't try something as dangerous as Fireball!"

"W-well, it's totally fine then. Astria is like a master when it comes to this stuff," Lesti said as she smacked her fist into her other palm like she had just gotten some bright idea, " She's already able to use four spells after just a week of training!" She puffed her chest out in pride and continued, "With her at my side, there's nothing to worry about. So, you can rest e-"

Smack!

I stared in shock at Lani's outstretched hand, which had just smacked Lesti straight across the face. Lesti cradled her reddening cheek in her palm, a mixture of shock and guilt on her face.

"You idiot!" Lani let her arm drop back to her side as tears started to form in her eyes, "You always act like this. You push yourself too far or do something dangerous and then laugh it off like it's nothing, keeping it hidden from me all the while. I know you have your reasons, but I wish you would rely on me more," she stepped forward and embraced Lesti lightly as tears started to roll down her cheeks, "I wouldn't be able to live with myself if something happened to you."

Lesti stood in her embrace for a long moment struggling with her own emotions. To me, it felt like she wanted to rely on Lani, but something was holding her back. In the end, she steeled her resolve and gently pushed Lani away.

"I'm sorry, Lani, but I have to do this on my own."

Lesti turned and walked out of the office without looking back. Lani crumpled to her knees as soon as she was out of sight. I started to turn and follow Lesti but turned back at the last minute. *I can't just leave her like this without saying anything.*

"Don't worry. I know she can be reckless, but I promise that I'll keep her safe no matter what. So, try not to worry, okay?"

Lani continued to stare listlessly at the ground, like a puppet whose strings had been cut. I waited a moment, but with no response in sight, I turned and left the room, hoping that my words would give her even the tiniest bit of solace.

* * *

Later that night, we were back in the classroom, practicing as usual. However, unlike before, I was providing light with the Magic Light spell. I had picked it up during a previous practice session since I thought it would be useful. Lesti could use it as well, but this way, she could conserve her magical energy for practice.

A magic circle was drawn on the board, but a few of the runes were still missing. According to Lesti, the circle in question was meant to create a blast of wind, and the missing pieces were the controls for power and direction. She was staring down at one of the few books on magical runes that she could get from the library, but I could tell her mind was elsewhere. She had been staring at the same page for five minutes now.

"You're losing focus again."

"N-no, I'm not. I was just trying to make sure I get the power output on this spell right."

She pointed to the missing runes in the magic circle on the board as if trying to prove her point.

"That's not going to fool me," I walked over and sat on top of the book, "It normally doesn't take you any time at all to decide how much power output a spell needs. And don't even try and tell me that this spell is more complicated than the others. I know better than that."

Having had her escape routes cut off, Lesti sat there, moving her mouth silently as she tried to come up with some other excuse.

"You were thinking about Lani, right? Why are you so against relying on her? She seems to care about you quite a bit, so I'm sure we could trust her."

"I know all that!" Lesti suddenly stood up and walked over to the window. After staring out into the darkness for a moment, she continued, "I know that Lani would do anything for me, and that's exactly the problem."

I walked to the end of the desk and looked out at the overcast night sky. Only a few stars peeked out from between the clouds. It almost felt like the sky was trying to match the gloomy mood around us. I let out a heavy sigh.

"I'm quite jealous, you know," I glanced to the side to observe Lesti, "You didn't even hesitate to try and use my power when you summoned me. Yet, you're worrying yourself silly over Lani. You must really care about her a lot."

"That's not true. I actually worried quite a bit in the beginning, you know?" she replied without looking at me, a faint smile playing on her lips, "As ashamed as I am to admit it, I only thought of familiars as a way to boost my own magical power at first. It wasn't until you got mad and yelled at me after class that I felt like I could rely on you a little. I realized that you were someone who wouldn't sacrifice themselves blindly for my sake."

"Of course not. Who would do that for some random girl that they barely know?" I asked jokingly as I broke my gaze away from the night sky to look at her directly, "Still, what makes you think that Lani would do that? I know she's kind of timid, but I never felt that she would throw her life away blindly."

Lesti closed her eyes and shook her head slightly, "That's not the kind of sacrifice I mean. You see, Lani and I are kind of like childhood friends. She was in the service of my parents for as long as I can remember. She's like a big sister to me, and I've always looked up to her. She was a really talented mage. So much so, that she was offered a position here when she was only eighteen."

For the first time since we had started talking, a smile crept over Lesti's face, and her voice picked up a little.

"You must have been really proud of her."

"Yeah! You should have seen her face when the headmistress herself showed up to try and recruit her. I don't think I've ever heard her stammer so much. She was so excited, but…"

Lesti turned to look at me for the first time since we started talking. The excitement and joy she had been expressing just a moment before faded, replaced by an expression full of pain and guilt.

"But then my parents died. When the news came, I was crushed. I didn't leave my room for an entire month. Lani turned down the instructor position here to stay with me. When I learned about that, I immediately stopped holing up in my room. I didn't want her to sacrifice such an amazing opportunity to take care of me. I told her that she should accept the position and that I would be fine, but even then, she refused to leave."

Lesti plopped down in the chair in front of me and rested her head on the cool wood of the desk. I walked around and laid on my side so that we were face to face.

"So, what did you do then?" I asked.

"I decided to come and join the magic academy. If Lani wouldn't listen to reason, then I would just have to get stronger, strong enough that she wouldn't need to sacrifice herself for me. I guess that was my original reason for getting stronger," she chuckled, "Sorry, I guess I told you a bit of a lie before."

"We'll call it payback for when I tried to hide what I had learned from Skell. Still, I think you might be misunderstanding something, Lesti." I moved my head closer to hers so that we were almost nose to nose.

"Oh, and what might that be?"

"You see, you've got it all backwards. Lani wasn't sacrificing herself for you. To her, you're far more important than being an instructor here at the academy. She stayed with you precisely because she didn't want to abandon someone who was so precious to her."

Lesti stared at me, eyes wide with disbelief. I was definitely making some assumptions here, but I didn't think they were wrong. If Lani cared more about her position as an instructor, she wouldn't have reacted to Lesti's unwillingness to rely on her so forcefully.

"I hadn't ever thought of it that way. I had always just assumed that I was keeping Lani from doing what she wanted," she closed her eyes as tears started to form in their corners, "I really hurt her today, didn't I?"

"Yeah, you probably did," I touched my nose to hers and closed my own eyes, " So, make sure you go and apologize to her tomorrow, okay?"

"Yeah."

After that, we sat there for a while, face to face, before returning to the dorm. We were both emotionally exhausted, and tomorrow was going to be another long day.

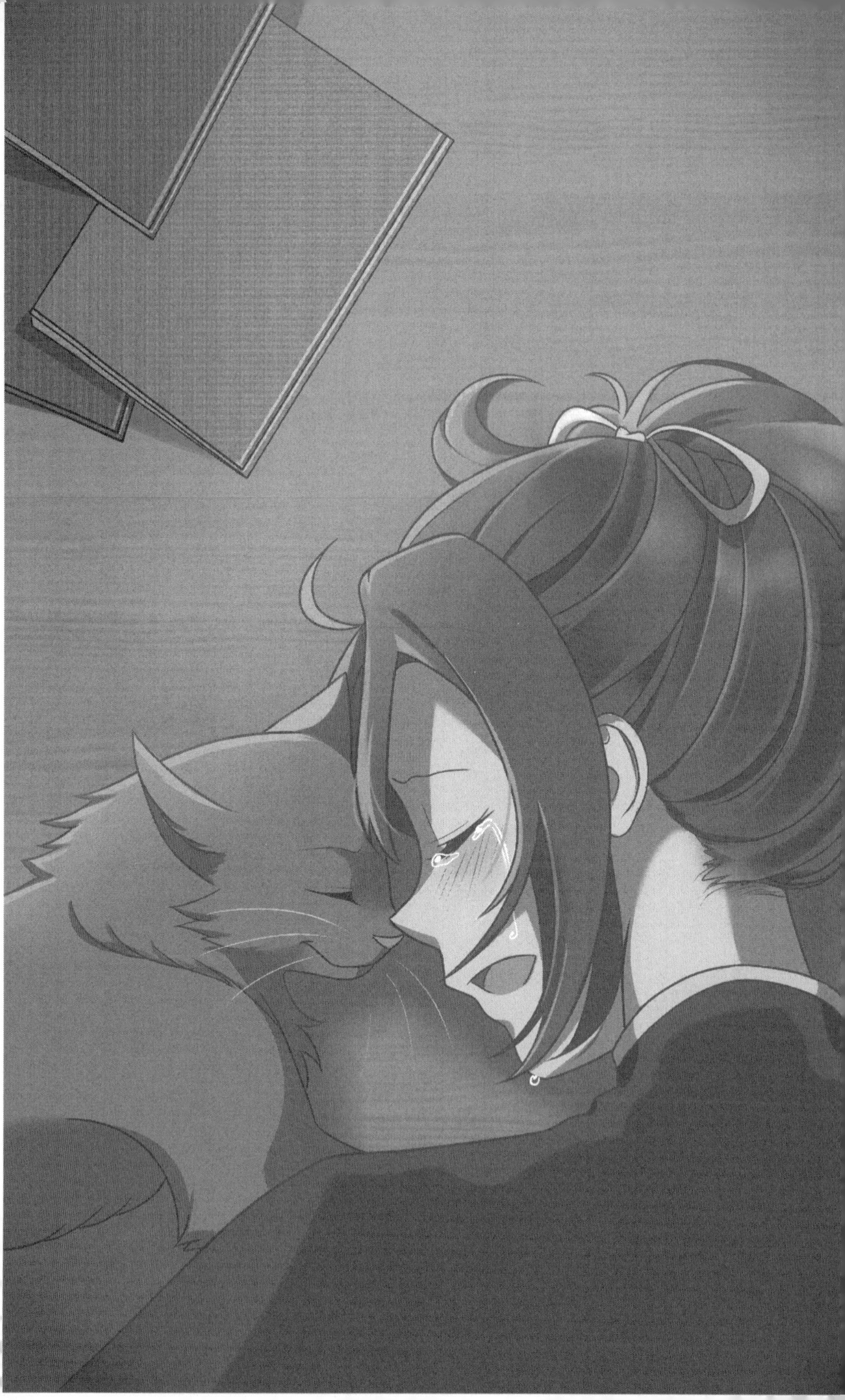

GROWTH AND RELATIONSHIPS

* * *

The next morning we found ourselves standing outside Lani's bedroom, bright and early. The sun had barely broken over the horizon, and the morning air still carried the cold of night. The hallways were empty for everyone except the kitchen staff, who had to rise early to prepare breakfast.

Lesti had dark circles under her eyes. I guess she had been worried about talking to Lani today because she had restlessly tossed and turned all night. I hadn't gotten much sleep myself, thanks to that. Still, I had to commend her. Despite how anxious she clearly was, she came here first thing in the morning to talk to Lani.

Lesti closed her eyes and took a deep breath, trying to prepare herself. Then, she raised her hand to knock on the door. However, when she did, the door swung open, and we found ourselves face to face with Lani.

"O-oh, Lani. Good morning," Lesti barely managed to sputter out a proper greeting.

"Good morning, Le-, Ms. Vilia. Did you need something?"

She appeared to be caught off guard at first but quickly switched to business mode. I'm guessing she hadn't been expecting us to be standing at her door first thing in the morning. Her eyes were still a little red from crying.

For Lesti's part, she couldn't seem to find her words now that the time had come. Her mouth opened and closed silently for a moment before she resorted to staring at her boots.

"If you don't need anything, then I'll be going. I have to prepare for today's lessons."

With that, Lani stepped past us, closing the door behind her and started to walk down the hallway. As the distance between us started to grow, I walked over to Lesti and bit her on the ankle, "Astria!? What are you doing?" Lesti's sudden outburst caused Lani to turn around and see what was going on. Meanwhile, I stared up at her with a defiant look on my face. *No way in hell am I letting you drag this out. Go get her!*

"Alright, alright, I get it," she let out a defeated sigh as she picked up on my thoughts and turned to face Lani.

Taking one last deep breath, she called out, "U-um, Lani? I'm really sorry about yesterday. I know you're always looking out for me and I, well, I really appreciate it," she turned her gaze away shyly, "It's just, I've always thought you were amazing and could accomplish so much, and I didn't want to be responsible for holding you back. So, I pushed you away, but I promise I won't do that anymore."

She paused for a moment as she slowly lifted her gaze up to peer at Lani, peeking out from beneath her bangs, "So, if it's alright with you, I'd like to show you what Astria and I've been working on. If you'll forgive me, that is?"

Lani stared back at us with an incomprehensible expression for a moment before turning and starting to walk away again. The look on Lesti's face was one of shock and disappointment. She hadn't been expecting Lani to turn her back on her after all that, and it showed.

A feeling of intense guilt washed over me. I had assured her that everything would be alright and pushed her to do this. I couldn't let things end here, after all that. I had to change Lani's mind even if it took a little force. I crouched down and got ready to dash after Lani, but to my surprise, she turned back and called to Lesti over her shoulder.

"Well, are you coming or not?"

Lesti and I both stared at her with baffled looks on our faces for a moment before she managed to utter a response.

"Where exactly are we going?"

A devilish smile played across Lani's face as she replied, "To my office, of course. We can't talk in the middle of the halls, now, can we?"

I breathed a sigh of relief, and Lesti ran up to Lani and thumped her fists playfully on her back, "I really thought you weren't going to forgive me!"

"Consider it payback for all the worry you've caused me so far," Lani turned around to face Lesti and flashed the first real smile I had seen her make since I had arrived in this world. It was a warm and inviting smile, full of love and kindness.

"Of course I forgive you, Lesti. You'll have to do much better than that to get rid of me. Now, let's get going, or else we're going to run out of time before classes. I have a lot of questions that I want to ask both of you, as well."

GROWTH AND RELATIONSHIPS

"Yeah. Let's go." Lesti replied, returning Lani's smile.

Watching the two walking away, I felt a strange mix of emotions. I was happy to see that things worked out between them, but at the same time I felt a little lonely. In this world, I didn't have any connections like that, and I would never see my friends from my old life again. And in my role as a familiar, it didn't look like I would really have the chance to forge those meaningful relationships here. Still, there was work to be done, so I pushed my feelings of loneliness aside and got ready to talk to Lani about Lesti's sudden growth as a mage.

Oliver

Two weeks later, we once again stood on the training grounds with the rest of Lesti's class. Lani was having the students practice defensive magic. She would launch a sphere of water at each student, and they had to use magic to block it. The only limitation was that they couldn't use fire magic. By this time, leaves had started to fall from the trees and were being blown all around the academy grounds. That made using fire magic dangerous.

"Earth Wall!"

Lesti's shout echoed across the training grounds as she finished her fake chant. The earth in front of her shot upwards and formed a wall, five feet thick and six feet high. The ball of water smacked into it harmlessly. The wall Lesti had made was clearly overkill. Unlike Skell, who had been merciless with his attacks against me, Lani was being careful to control her output to avoid hurting the students.

Lesti stood there and proudly took in her work, "That's a fantastic Earth Wall spell if I've ever seen one!"

The reaction from her fellow students wasn't one of admiration, however. Many of them scoffed and threw angry glances in my direction. Over the last two weeks, Lesti had shot up to be the top performer in her class by a landslide. Most of the students seemed to think that her sudden spike in power and ability was because of me. I even heard some of them accuse her of being a cheater.

Well, I guess they aren't totally wrong on that front. She's got a massive advantage over the others since they can't use instruction-based magic. It doesn't help that she keeps bragging like that, either.

"Very good, Ms. Vilia," Lani called out from somewhere on the other side of the wall, "Now, could you please return the grounds to normal, so we can move on to the next student?"

"Oh, right. Release!" Lesti waved her hand dismissively, and the earth wall receded back into the ground. After that, she returned to sit by me with the rest of the students.

"Right, Who's next?" Lani continued without grading Lesti any further. There wasn't really any point after all. She couldn't give any real feedback in front of the other students since they might figure out what we were doing. She looked over the rest of the students, "Is that everyone?"

"Instructor, Oliver hasn't gone yet," Sebastian's familiar voice called out from the crowd.

"Oh, Oliver, my apologies," Lani stood on her toes and peered at a boy in the back, "I didn't see you in the back there. Please, come up and show me your best defensive spell."

"Yeah, Oliver, show us what you can do," Sebastian's lackeys started to chuckle until he shot them a harsh glare. *That's odd. Normally, Sebastian would be chuckling right along with them.*

Oliver stood up from his hiding spot in the back of the class and made his way to the front. He was one of the shorter boys in the class, which was why he had almost avoided getting called on. His chestnut-colored hair was cut short, which was unusual for a student of the academy.

His brown eyes were downcast during his entire walk to the front of the class. As he passed by Lesti, she gave him a thumbs up in an attempt to encourage him, but he either didn't see her or chose to ignore her. To me, he seemed to be rather nervous.

I wonder if that has something to do with Sebastian calling him out. I glanced over in his direction to see him watching Oliver with an amused look on his face. *Well, that can't be good.* Sebastian had been exceptionally irritable since I had turned him down, and Lesti had started to outperform him in practice lessons. Seeing him enjoying himself once again could only mean trouble.

"Alright, remember, this is practice, so there's no reason to be nervous,"

Lani called out to Oliver once he was in position, "Go ahead and start your incantation."

With that, Lani began to slowly recite her own incantation. Oliver continued to stand there for a few moments before realizing that she had begun. When he finally realized what was going on, he panicked unnecessarily and began reciting rapidly.

I watched his magical energy swirl chaotically around him as it tried to figure out his intent. Between his rushed incantation and his panicked state of mind, he must have been having trouble forming a clear image. From what I could see, it seemed like he was trying to imitate Lesti's Earth Wall spell.

In most cases, it would have been an excellent choice. Earth Wall was an extremely easy spell to perform with imaging due to its simple nature. The abundance of dirt and rocks on the training ground only simplified things further. However, when panicking like that, almost every spell was guaranteed to fail.

"Aqua Sphere!" Lani finished and fired her spell at Oliver. It wasn't traveling incredibly fast, but the sight of the sphere caused him to panic further.

"E-Earth Wall!" He finished his chant, and a wall of dirt formed in front of him. However, unlike when Lesti cast it, the wall wasn't solid and was too thin. The sphere of water crashed into the loose dirt, transforming it into mud and sending it splattering all over Oliver.

Lani ran up to him as he wiped the muck off his face with his hand, "Are you alright? Here, let me help," She pulled a handkerchief from her pocket and started trying to wipe his face. Seeing Oliver treated like a child, a wave of giggles passed through the class. Hearing this, he pushed Lani's hand away and stepped back.

"I'll take care of it myself," He then walked off toward the school building.

Lani looked after the young man with a worried look on her face but didn't stop him from leaving. Besides, she didn't have any real reason to stop him. Since he was the last student, the class would be dismissed soon. Plus, it wasn't likely that any feedback on his spell casting was going to get through to him right now. By letting him go early, she also gave him a chance to escape the worst of the ridicule.

"Alright, I think that's everyone," Lani turned back and started addressing the class with a forced smile on her face, "Let's review what we learned today before we go."

As Lani jumped into her end of class review session, I heard Lesti's voice in my head, "Let's go check on Oliver after class. I'm worried about him."

I turned to look at Lesti, cocking my head to the side, "That's unusual. I think this is the first time I've seen you take an interest in one of your fellow students," my tail twitched mischievously as I decided to tease her a little, "Do you have a crush on him or something?"

Lesti tossed an annoyed glance in my direction, "Haha. Very funny. No, I don't have a crush on him," she paused for a moment considering her words, "I'm just worried is all."

I didn't buy her explanation, but I didn't want to pry. I remembered when I was her age, and nothing pushed me away more than someone coercing me to express my feelings about someone before I was ready. Whatever her reasoning, I was glad we were checking in on Oliver, "I think it's a good idea to check on him. If I'm being honest, I'm rather worried myself," I glanced over at Sebastian, who was sitting there with his usual smug expression on his face.

"Thanks, Astria."

As soon as Lani finished her review, we headed toward the school building in search of Oliver.

* * *

"He's not here, huh?" Lesti looked around with a perplexed look on her face, "I was sure he would have been at the well cleaning up."

Lesti and I were standing by the well that was located on the west side of the school building. We decided to start our search for Oliver here because it was often used by students when they needed water for personal use. That made it the perfect place to clean the mud off.

"He did have a good head start on us. Maybe he finished cleaning up and went back to his room?"

"It is rather chilly out today," Lesti replied, "Staying out here while wet would be a good way to catch a cold, so that might be where he went. We can't really go into the boys' dorm, though," Lesti closed her eyes in thought and folded her arms across her chest, "I guess we could search the school building? It's so large, though. Where would we even start?" she continued muttering to herself as we started to wander toward the rear entrance to the school.

As we rounded the corner, I glanced over in the direction of the dorms to see if I could spot Oliver. The lawn was entirely empty, and I expected the dorms were the same. Most of the students were somewhere in the school building, either studying, practicing, or consulting with their instructors to prepare for the upcoming practical exam. *Still, I doubt Oliver would have gone to any of the usual places after what happened on the training grounds. There'd be too many people around. His room is probably the best bet.*

"Astria, look over there," Lesti nudged me with the side of her foot to get my attention. She was pointing towards the rear entrance to the school where Sebastian and his lackeys had just emerged from. *What are they doing here? Shouldn't they be preparing for the ex-?* Suddenly, I was swept off my feet by Lesti as she ducked back around the corner.

"Hey! What are you doing?" I struggled to free myself from her grip.

"Shhh!" Lesti held a finger to her lips, motioning for me to be quiet.

"Why are you shushing me!?" I glared at her as I flicked my tail wildly in agitation, "You're the only one who can hear me right now, you know?"

"Oh, right. Sorry, I got carried away," Lesti apologized as she peered around the corner, "I just didn't want them to see us."

"Huh? Why not?" I peered around the corner to see what had caused Lesti to hide like that, "Wait, why is Oliver with them!?"

I hadn't noticed before because of his height, but Oliver was mixed in the middle of Sebastian and his two companions. I expected him to still be upset, but from here, it looked like he was in a rather good mood. He was talking to Sebastian and the others with a smile on his face.

We watched them as they crossed the lawn toward the dorms. Once the group was blocked from our line of vision by the boys' dorm, we made a mad dash toward the corner of the building and cautiously peeked around it. What we saw was rather unexpected. Rather than entering the boys' dorm, they kept going straight toward the old annex building where I was originally summoned.

"What are they going to the old annex for?" I asked, looking up at Lesti, "There isn't anything in there, right?"

She shook her head, "No, nothing useful anyway. I gave the place a good looking over while I was working on the summoning ritual and didn't find anything."

"Hmm. Then, what could they be doing?" I turned my gaze back to the group of boys, "Oh, look. They're going around the building."

While we were talking, the group of boys had started to change course and were now headed for the side of the building. We continued to follow them, hopping from hiding place to hiding place until they came to a stop behind the annex building. We peered around the corner of the building, doing our best to stay hidden.

What the heck are they doing back here? There was nothing of note behind the annex building. In fact, the only thing that I could say about the space is that it was well hidden. Since there was nothing here, no one would bother to come all the way back here normally. However, it was the perfect place to go if you wanted to avoid prying eyes. *I have a bad feeling about this.*

Oliver was standing with his back to the wall, while Sebastian and his two lackeys stood in a semicircle facing him. Everybody was still smiling, but I wasn't sure that would last much longer. I had seen too many scenes like this during my previous life. Kids didn't go to a hidden place like this unless they were up to no good.

Eventually, Sebastian and his group backed up and stood a good distance from Oliver. Then, they all began chanting. I watched as the magic swirled around all four of them. The two boys with Sebastian were gathering dirt and water together to form small balls of mud. Meanwhile, Sebastian himself was casting some sort of wind-based spell I hadn't seen before.

Oliver, for his part, was casting the Earth Wall spell that he had attempted to use earlier in the day. Since he was much calmer now, the spell was working as intended. A well-formed wall of packed earth took shape before him. It wasn't as impressive as what Lesti had done, but it would still be enough to block the simple mud balls that were about to be launched at him.

However, before that could happen, Sebastian unleashed his spell. A powerful gust of condensed air shot towards the wall. It had enough force that on impact, the wall crumbled. The other two boys adjusted their aim and launched their mud balls right through the gap. They both slammed into Oliver, covering him in mud and knocking him off his feet.

Upon seeing this, Lesti leapt from her place in hiding and ran over to stand between Oliver and the other boys with me hot on her heels.

"Knock it off!" she yelled while glaring at Sebastian.

"Lesti? What are you doing here?" Sebastian looked at us with his usual smug smile and waved a hand as if trying to brush us aside, "If you could move aside, you're getting in the way of our exam practice."

"Exam practice!? Don't give me that crap!" Lesti pointed to Oliver on the ground behind her, "This is nothing more than simple bullying!"

"I don't know what gave you that idea. We're just being good classmates. We saw that our friend Oliver was struggling with his defensive spells, so we offered to help him practice," Sebastian leaned to the side to look around Lesti at Oliver, "You did want our help, didn't you Oliver?"

"Y-Yeah. That's right," Oliver responded without looking up.

"Oliver," Lesti turned around and looked down at the boy, a look of pity on her face, "You don't have to do this, you know. I could help you practice."

For the first time, Oliver looked up at her. However, the look on his face wasn't anything like what I had expected to see.

"What could you possibly teach me? How to cheat?" Oliver lashed out at Lesti, his face scrunched up in anger, "Or maybe how to use your noble privilege to get away with breaking academy rules? A commoner like me would have been thrown out if I had done even a fraction of the things you did!" Oliver stood up so that he was face to face with Lesti, "Don't act like some sort of hero. If anything, you're the villain here."

With his piece said, Oliver turned and walked off in a huff, leaving Lesti standing there in a state of shock.

"Well, there you have it," Sebastian shrugged his shoulders and looked at Lesti in mock disappointment, "Looks like he doesn't want the help of a cheater like you."

"I-I'm not a cheater!" Lesti wheeled around to face Sebastian.

"Oh, so what would you call summoning a familiar without permission?" Sebastian walked closer till he was nearly nose to nose with Lesti, "Oliver's right, a normal student would have been kicked out," He then leaned in and whispered something in her ear that I couldn't hear with a sadistic smile on his face.

When he pulled away, Lesti's expression had turned from one of hurt to one of anger. Her eyes were filled with hatred for the boy standing before her.

"Oh, looks like I've overstayed my welcome." Sebastian turned and walked away after Oliver, calling over his shoulder to his companions, "Let's go."

Lesti glared at his back as if she were trying to bore a hole into it until he rounded the corner. Once he was gone, she backed up to the wall behind her and sank down to the ground. I walked over and rubbed against her in an attempt to comfort her and asked, "What did Sebastian say to you to upset you so much? You normally don't let him get under your skin like that."

Lesti stared off into space for a moment before answering, "He said that my parents would be proud."

"I'm surprised you didn't punch him on the spot," I swatted a nearby rock sending it tumbling across the ground, "He had it coming after saying something like that. Want me to go claw his eyes out for you?"

"Hey, don't go making my self-control be for naught," She smiled at my joke, but then quickly turned serious again, "I honestly would have punched him without a second thought if we weren't both nobles. Injuring him could start a feud between our families. If his father used his clout in the alliance, he could easily stop most of the trade coming into our territory. At the end of the day, I would just be making my people suffer for my own self-satisfaction."

"He wasn't wrong, you know," I looked Lesti right in the eye, "Your parents really would be proud of how you put your people first."

I saw the anger drain from her face, replaced by a happy smile, "Yeah.

Thank you, Astria." She stood up and stretched before looking back down at me with her usual vigor, "Well, I feel a lot better. What do you say we go and get some dinner?"

I shook my head, "You go on ahead. I have something that I need to take care of. I'll catch up with you in the usual place this evening."

"Alright, just promise me you won't do anything crazy, alright?" Lesti replied with a worried look on her face.

"Don't worry. I promise I won't," With that, I dashed off to find Lani.

* * *

I found Lani in her office, staring at a piece of paper and tapping her finger absentmindedly. Whatever was on her mind was clearly distracting her as she didn't even notice me enter the room. It took me jumping up onto her desk before she finally noticed me.

"Oh, Astria. Sorry, I didn't see you there." She acknowledged me half-heartedly as she got up and closed the door to the office, "Did you need something?"

"Did I come at a bad time?" I found a comfortable stack of papers to sit on as Lani returned to her seat, "You seem distracted."

"Oh, that," She let out a heavy sigh, "I'm just thinking about earlier today is all."

"You mean the incident with Oliver?"

She nodded, "That's right. I'm worried about him. He seemed panicked when he was casting his spell. Oliver is usually very consistent and stable with his spell casting. Something must have happened to rattle him like that."

The image of Oliver calmly casting his spell behind the old annex flashed through my mind.

"Actually, I came here to ask you about Oliver. I also felt like something wasn't quite right, but I don't really know anything about him. Can you tell me anything?"

"You were worried, too, huh?" Lani leaned back in her chair and stared at the ceiling, "Where should I start? I guess the first thing you should know is

OLIVER

that Oliver is one of the few commoners here at our academy. He was sent at the behest of the lord of the territory his family lives in."

"Which territory would that be? Not Sebastian's, I hope?" My tail flicked about wildly at the mere thought.

"Oliver isn't from Sebastian's family territory. If I remember correctly, his father is a merchant whose base of operations is in the Dawster Family's territory."

Lani went over to a nearby bookshelf and pulled out a large folded sheet of paper. She unfolded it carefully on her desk, revealing a map of the alliance and its various territories. She pointed to a particularly large territory near the north side of the alliance.

"This is the Dawster territory," She then pointed to a smaller neighboring territory along the coast, "It's right next to the Vilia territory that Lesti comes from."

"Oh, so they're neighbors. Does that mean they have good relations?"

"Unfortunately, no. While their relations aren't terrible, I'd call them neutral at best. They trade and get along well enough, but the families have never liked each other."

I cocked my head to the side, "Why's that? Wouldn't it be more beneficial for them to get along?"

"You're partially right," Lani replied with a slightly pained smile on her face, "However, there's always been a power imbalance between the two territories. The Dawster territory is large and has an abundance of raw materials, so it can mostly provide for itself. The Vilia territory, on the other hand, is heavily reliant on trade."

"I see how that could be a problem, but what does all of this have to do with Oliver?"

"Well, there's one more reason the two families don't get along well. They have different opinions on how to treat their citizens. The Dawster family has put in place a strict class system based on what type of work you perform. Any work that buys them clout in the alliance is seen as more valuable and is rewarded as such. Being a merchant is one of the most valued jobs."

"Being a merchant is? Didn't you just say that the Dawster territory didn't need to trade that much?"

"That's right. However, they're able to use their merchants and abundant resources to buy a lot of favors from the more influential families in the alliance." Lani slumped back down in her chair, "Being a merchant is so popular that they had to implement a licensing system to limit the numbers. That means that if you lose your license, then you lose your livelihood as a merchant."

"So, you think that Oliver's family might be at risk of losing their license?" I closed my eyes while trying to piece everything together, "That doesn't make any sense, though. Oliver has been doing fine at the academy all this time. Why would he suddenly have to worry about his family losing their license?"

Lani shook her head, "For all I know, the license has nothing to do with Oliver's behavior. I just can't think of anything else that he would be so worried about. He's always been a very consistent student, though he was never very high in the class rankings."

The memory of Oliver lashing out at Lesti behind the old annex flashed through my mind, "I wonder if he's just jealous of Lesti's newfound success. Did he ever seem like the jealous type to you?"

"Hmm," Lani looked up at the ceiling in thought for a moment before replying, "I don't think so. He never really seemed to care about his ranking all that much. What makes you think that?"

I explained what happened earlier in the day to Lani.

"I can't believe Oliver would say something like that to her," Lani seemed genuinely surprised that Oliver had accused Lesti of abusing her privilege, "He's always been so quiet and easy-going. Though, I guess I've never seen him really interacting with the other students in the class."

"So, you don't have any ideas about why he might have said that?"

"Unfortunately, no. I don't really know much about Oliver's past. I've only known him as a student of the academy."

"Well, I won't waste any more of your time then," I got up and hopped off the desk, heading for the door, "Thanks for the information."

"What are you going to do now?" Lani got up and walked around her desk to open the door for me.

"I'm going to start investigating. I need to learn more about Oliver's situation if I'm going to understand why he's acting this way."

"And how exactly are you going to do that?" Lani folded her arms across her chest as she glared at me, "I hope I don't have to remind you that you aren't allowed to leave the academy grounds."

"Oh, I don't need to leave the academy grounds," I glanced up at Lani before making my way out of the room, "I've got the world's best source of information on Oliver right here after all."

Ambush

I was sitting in one of the old classrooms on the second floor of the school's south wing. Like many of the other rooms in this wing, this classroom was currently being used as storage. The entire room was covered in a thick layer of dust that would get kicked up whenever I moved around too much. Tonight was finally the night that I would put my plan into action.

It had been a few days since the initial incident with Oliver had occurred on the training grounds. I spent those days learning Oliver's habits and patterns so that I could eventually corner him when he was alone. Oliver would walk through this hall every night on his way to the practice classrooms in the east wing. So, I laid in ambush inside this dark and dusty room.

The plan was to catch Oliver off guard and pull him into this room with magic. Once he was in, I would shut the door, locking him in complete darkness. Then, while he was scrambling to cast a spell to light the room, I would transform into my tiger form. I still couldn't turn into a full-sized tiger, but at this point, I could maintain a young adult form for a few minutes. Oliver would finally get the light on and be faced with a giant talking tiger. He wouldn't recognize me, and he'd be too terrified to not answer my questions. It was a perfect plan. I sat in the dusty room and stared out into the dark hallway, waiting for my target to pass by.

The only thing that had me worried was the familiar feeling of being watched. Somewhere in the room was the same presence that had been spying on me since shortly after I had arrived in this world. I didn't bother trying to spot it anymore. Every time I tried it would disappear without a trace. Besides, it didn't seem interested in getting involved, only ever watching from nearby.

More and more time passed with just me and my invisible stalker until I began to worry that Oliver might not be coming. *Hmm. Is he not going to practice tonight? I figured he'd be going every night with exams coming up so soon.*

Then, just as I was about to give up for the night, I heard footsteps coming down the hall. I crouched down and did my best to control my tail as it twitched about excitedly. Soon, a light appeared out in the hallway, casting large shadows. I prepared my counter magic so that I could snuff the light. I would have to act fast. There would only be a single moment where my target was in range.

The light and the sound of the footsteps grew closer and closer until they were right outside the room. Then, at the moment the person first appeared in my vision, I snuffed the light and cast a new spell I had learned with the help of Lesti, Wind Rake. A powerful gust of wind, strong enough to knock a grown adult off their feet materialized and slammed into my target, pulling them toward me. They tumbled through the door, which I quickly shut with another Wind Rake.

I jumped into position and reared up on my hind legs, raising my front paws above my head and opening my mouth like I was going to roar. I began focusing on my transformation into a tiger, but that wasn't to be. My target reacted far quicker than I could have anticipated. They rolled to their feet in the darkness with a single smooth motion and instantly cast the Magic Light spell.

With the light returned to the room, I found myself face to face with Lani. She was crouched low in a ready stance and had a serious expression on her face. I froze in horror as I realized that I had snagged the wrong target.

"H-Huh? Astria?" Her face turned to one of absolute confusion as she saw me standing there like some sort of stuffed animal statue, "W-What's going on? Why are you standing like that?"

I slowly lowered myself back down onto my front paws, "This is…a test," I said the first thing that came to my mind.

Lani looked at me like I was speaking a different language, "A-A test?"

"Yeah, that's right," I averted my gaze, pretending to inspect the various piles of junk in the room, "I wanted to make sure that you were prepared for an ambush. You never know when an enemy could be lurking around the corner."

"Is that so?" I felt a chill shoot down my spine. Glancing over at Lani, I saw that she had the same smile on her face that she had when Lesti had first used instruction based magic in front of her, "Astria, is there something you would like to tell me?"

"Y-Yes, Ma'am," I hung my head in defeat. *Why is Lani so scary when she's mad!?* I spent the next several minutes explaining how I had been planning to ambush Oliver and extract information from him. By the time I had finished, Lani was rubbing her temples like she had a headache.

"So, let me get this straight. You were planning to ambush a student and threaten to beat him up if he didn't answer your questions?"

I glanced up at Lani without raising my head, "I thought it was a pretty good plan."

"In what way is that a good plan!?" Lani finally lost her cool completely, "You can't just go around ambushing students! We're going to find Lesti, and the two of you are going back to the dorms right this instant."

"I can't give up yet. I still haven't gotten any information!" I finally raised my head and protested, "If I don't find anything, then Lesti won't be able to focus on her practical exam. Is that what you want?"

"W-Well, when you put it that way," Lani hesitated for a moment when I brought up Lesti.

"Rather than have Lesti running all over the school, isn't it better to have me looking into this matter?" I stood up straight on put on my best politician's voice, doing my best to sound as convincing and sincere as possible, "I promise that I'll give up on ambushing him. So, please let me keep investigating a while longer, for Lesti's sake?"

"O-Oh, fine!" The last of Lani's defenses broke down at my pleading. She really did have a soft spot for Lesti, "You had better keep your promise, though. If I find out you ambushed another student, I'll make you wish you had gone back to the dorm."

AMBUSH

"I promise. I wouldn't lie to you about this Lani," I really meant it too. The last thing I wanted was to make her angry when I didn't need to. I'd just have to get my information some other way, "Well, if there's nothing else, then I need to get back to searching for Oliver."

"Oh, if you're looking for him, I saw him going into one of the self-study rooms earlier. I told him not to stay too late, so I'm not sure if he's still there."

"Alright, I'll go check that out," I used a series of Wind Rake spells to get the door open, "Thanks, Lani. Sorry for ambushing you!"

I then dashed down the hall without waiting for a response.

* * *

After wandering through the dark halls for a while, I eventually made my way to the west wing, where the library and self-study rooms were located. In my hurry to escape from Lani before she could change her mind, I had forgotten to ask her which floor Oliver had been on. So, I was currently standing at the stairwell on the second floor, trying to decide if I should go up or down. *I guess I'll start with the third floor. That way, I don't have to climb as many stairs.*

However, right as I reached my decision, the first indication of someone approaching reached my ears as footsteps echoed down the stairwell. I quickly dashed into an empty self-study room nearby and peeked out through the crack in the door. The sound grew louder, and candlelight began filtering down from the top of the staircase. Soon after, Oliver and Sebastian rounded the corner and came down the stairs, stopping on the landing right outside the room I was hiding in.

"Well then, I'll be heading to bed," Sebastian said as he patted Oliver on the shoulder, "Don't work too late. Making a mistake with this kind of magic isn't something you walk away from. It's better to have your wits about you."

I felt my jaw go slack at the sight of Sebastian being so friendly with Oliver. *Is this really the same kid that was pummeling him with spells just a few days ago?*

"I know, but I need to hurry," Oliver smiled back at Sebastian, "This will all be for nothing if I don't complete the ritual before practical exams."

"I guess that's true. Well, I'm sure you can pull it off. Just don't forget about me once everything is said and done," Sebastian's face grew slightly more serious, "I'll be counting on you to keep up your end of the bargain."

"Of course, I would never dream of letting you down after everything you've done for me. Still," Oliver looked down at his feet with a worried expression for a moment before raising his gaze to meet Sebastian's, "You're sure that I won't get expelled for this, right?"

Sebastian reached out and grabbed Oliver's shoulder, giving him a firm shake, "Of course not. They didn't kick out that failure Lesti after she summoned the fleabag, right? With my connections, there's no way you'll get expelled. Trust me."

"Yeah. I do. It's just, I feel weird doing this after I yelled at her like that the other day. Like-."

"Hey, hey. We talked about this already. You don't need to feel guilty about this. You're not like her. What we're doing here is just leveling the playing field. After all, you're doing this all by your own power. I'm sure she had the help of that failure of an Instructor. It's totally different, okay?"

"Y-Yeah. Yeah, you're right," I saw the doubt and fear clear from Oliver's face. *Well, I guess Sebastian can be a pretty smooth talker when he wants to be. Still, I have a bad feeling about this. I had better figure out what they're doing and fast. Practical exams are right around the corner.*

The boys finished saying their goodbyes after that and parted ways. Once they were both out of sight, I set out after Oliver, who had gone into the library. I followed him through the library, dashing from bookshelf to bookshelf until we reached an area that had very low foot traffic. I felt my heart start to sink into my stomach when I recognized where we were. The section contained almost all of the limited number of books the school had on magic circles.

Oliver looked through the books for a few minutes, occasionally grabbing one and flipping through its pages. Eventually, he found what he was looking for and headed for the front desk. The librarian was packing up for the night and looked annoyed at being bothered so late but still let him check the book out.

After leaving the library, I spent another fifteen minutes following Oliver through the school building as he seemed to wander around aimlessly. *Is he trying to avoid being followed or something?* We had finally made our way to the south exit of the school, and Oliver was peeking around the corner suspiciously. Once the coast was clear, he slipped out the door, and I followed him into the night.

* * *

After following Oliver for a while, I saw him sneaking into the old annex building where Lesti had first summoned me. Unfortunately, he had closed the door behind him, which meant I couldn't follow immediately without giving myself away. I waited for a bit before I carefully used magic to open the door as quietly as possible. Once inside, I looked down the first-floor hall but didn't see any sign of Oliver.

Hopefully, he didn't hear me coming in. He might have snuffed his light if he did.

After giving it some thought, I decided to start my search on the second floor. I hopped up the stairs as swiftly and quietly as I could. Fortunately, I was very light, so the old weathered floor and stairs barely made a noise as I made my way up to the second floor.

Upon reaching the top, I poked my head around the corner and peered down the hallway. Unlike the night on which I had first been brought to this world, it was gloomy and overcast. Very little light made its way inside from the large windows on the front of the building. I had expected to see some sort of light leaking out from one of the classrooms, but the hallway was completely dark.

I walked down the hall, being careful to check out each door that I went by. It was obvious that someone had opened each one recently. The dust had been cleared away at the entrance to each room, and I could see footprints going to and fro.

I doubt all of this is from when Lesti was exploring this building. The dust would have settled again after such a long time. Was it Oliver? Why would he have gone through all the rooms? Lesti said there wasn't anything important here when she searched the place.

Remembering what Lesti said caused me to pause. *Lesti had said there was nothing important in here when she searched the place. That's not true anymore, though. There's something really important right down this hall.* I looked down the hall at one particularly familiar door. Behind that door was the magic circle that was used to summon me.

I slowly made my way further down the hall, doing my best not to make a noise. I had asked Lesti about the circle once before. She said that the teachers had made sure to destroy it so that no other students could use it. *If that's the case, why would Oliver be here?* My mind flashed back to the book he had borrowed from the library just before heading here. *It couldn't be...*

I finally drew close to the door and found that it was cracked ever so slightly. I paused and listened carefully but couldn't hear any noise coming from within the room. No candlelight flickered on the other side of the barrier, leaving the inside of the room pitch black. After a moment, I squeezed through the small opening into the darkness on the other side of the doorway.

Even with my feline vision, I could hardly see when I first entered the room, causing me to pause at the entrance. As my eyes adjusted, I saw what I had feared most in the middle of the room, a nearly complete magic circle. A wave of nostalgia passed over me as I slowly made my way toward the circle.

He really was rebuilding it, then. It looks like he hasn't finished, though. The circle on the ground before me was nearly identical to the one that had been used to summon me to this world. However, there were some minor differences in the runes, and some were missing altogether.

I moved into the circle to get a better look around the rest of the room. In the several weeks since I had been summoned, I had gotten used to being a cat. Even now, I could remember how big everything had felt when I first arrived and how hard it had been to do something as simple as walk. Yet, the room now felt normal to me, and moving about was as natural as could be.

As I sat there, awash in nostalgia, I heard the floorboards creak behind me. I wheeled around at the noise, but I was too late. Upon turning around, my face was covered by a thick cloth. Whoever was holding it dove to the ground and grabbed hold of me. The cloth had a strange, sweet scent to it.

Power Cat! I immediately activated my power boost spell and forced my assailant away, jumping back. With some distance between us, I could see that it was Oliver. He must have been hiding in the darkest corner of the room when I came in. My fur stood on end as I stared him down.

"It's okay, I don't want to hurt you," Oliver said in a sickly-sweet voice like one might use with any scared animal. He held his hand out to me and repositioned himself between me and the door, "I can't let you go back to your master after you've seen this, though."

Yeah. That's not gonna happen. With Power Cat and Speed Boost, there's no way you're stopping me from getting by. Speed Boost! I activated the spell and moved to dash past Oliver. However, as soon as I moved, my vision blurred, and I tripped over my own feet and fell on my side. *What's going on? My body feels heavy. Crap, was it that cloth?*

I glanced over at Oliver and saw his body relax. He approached me with the drugged cloth in hand.

"Sorry about this, but I need to make sure you stay out for a while," Oliver reached down and placed the cloth over my nose and mouth again. The world around me blurred and twisted until I lost consciousness completely.

* * *

I woke up to the flickering light of a single candle before me. My vision was still blurry, and my body still heavy. I could hear two voices in the room with me. When I glanced over, I saw it was Oliver and Sebastian. With the little strength I had, I tried to reach out to Lesti. I was so groggy, I wasn't sure if I was even doing it right, or if she heard me at all.

"Please, get here fast! I need you!"

I stopped calling out to Lesti as soon as I heard the boys talking. I needed to wake up. I needed to get out of here, but my body was so heavy. If Lesti didn't hear me, I had a sick feeling that things were going to get grim for me rather quickly.

"You fool. I can't believe you let yourself be followed," Sebastian was berating Oliver, neither realizing that I was awake, "The whole plan is ruined now."

"I-It's not ruined. I can still complete the ritual. I just need more time."

"There is no more time, you peasant!" Sebastian began yelling at Oliver, "How can you not understand that!?"

"W-What are you saying? I captured her familiar," Oliver began to shake, "If we just keep her hidden for a while, it shouldn't be impossible to finish the ritual!"

"You really don't know anything, do you? Familiars can communicate with their master up to a mile away! As soon as the fleabag wakes up," Sebastian paused, a thoughtful expression crawling over his face, "Wait, wait. There may be a way to fix this, after all."

"Really!?" Oliver's eyes lit up with hope for the first time since I had begun watching their exchange.

"It's rather simple, my dear Oliver," Sebastian reached out and patted him on the shoulder, "We just have to make sure the little fleabag doesn't wake up."

A confused look came over Oliver's face, "You mean the sleeping drug? I doubt we have enough to keep her out for that long."

"Well, if we don't have enough left, then that only leaves us with one choice, then, doesn't it?" Sebastian walked over to the nearby desk and picked up a small knife. A chill ran down my spine as I realized what Sebastian was thinking about doing.

Oliver's eyes went wide as he came to the same realization as me, "Sebastian, you can't be serious."

"What? You're going to get cold feet on me now?" Sebastian glared at Oliver, "If this gets out, then your family is done. Your father's merchant license will be revoked. Your entire family will sink into poverty, and that's if they're lucky. Lord Dawster might just have you all hung for bringing shame to his family."

Oliver's face turned pale at Sebastian's threats, but he didn't back down. He stepped between Sebastian and me, blocking his path.

"Still, I can't take part in this. The only reason that I went along with your plan was that I thought it was the only way to protect my family. However, I won't take part in murder, and I won't stand by and watch you do it either."

Sebastian's expression grew dark, and magic started to flow around him, "You filthy commoner. You would dare defy me? After everything that I've done for you, you would stand in my way?"

"I'm sorry. I really do appreciate you trying to help me, but I can't let you do this," Oliver stood his ground. I had to give it to the boy. He had more guts than I had given him credit for.

"I see. Fine then, have it your way," Sebastian's expression softened, and his shoulders relaxed. Oliver let his guard down, probably thinking that Sebastian was backing down. However, I could still see Sebastian's magic swirling around him.

"Air Blast!" A ball of condensed air slammed into the unprepared Oliver, sending him tumbling to the ground. He landed at the far edge of the magic circle, and his head bounced hard off the stone floor, knocking him unconscious.

With Oliver out of the way, Sebastian turned his attention to me. At first, he approached slowly, taking his time. However, his eyes quickly went wide as soon as he realized I was awake. He dashed across the room, lifting the knife over his head.

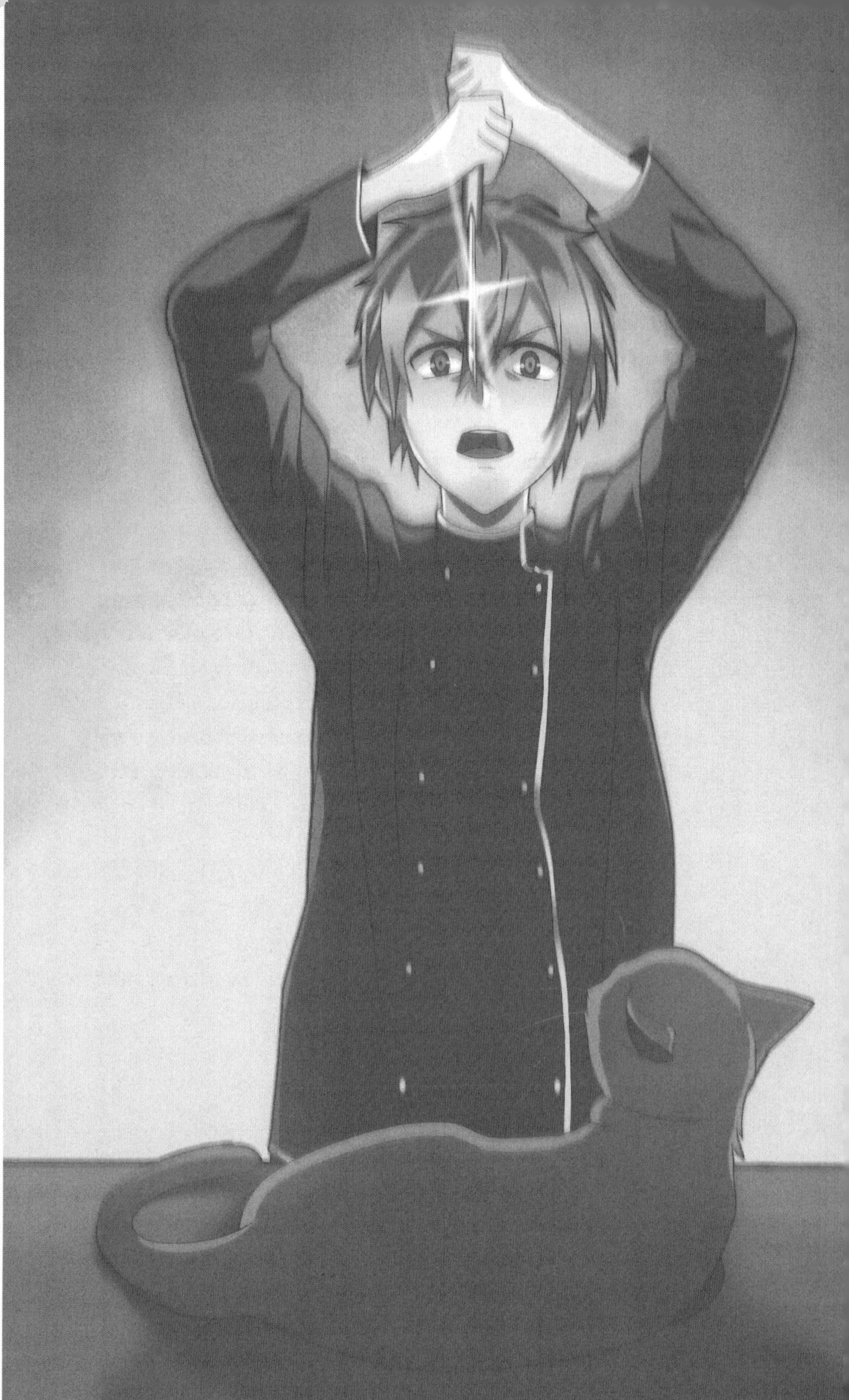

AMBUSH

I tried to move, but my body was still heavy, and I couldn't get my feet under me. Realizing that I wouldn't be able to dodge, I quickly threw up a barrier spell. Sebastian quickly closed the gap and brought the knife down hard, slamming it into my barrier.

I wasn't sure what drug they had used, but it was also affecting my ability to use magic. Normally, a physical attack like this would have been nothing, but it was taking everything I had just to keep the barrier up. Sebastian raised the knife overhead repeatedly, slamming it back down into my barrier each time.

What little magical strength I had was slowly being sapped away. My mind raced as I tried to find some way of escaping or buying more time. I couldn't use any attack spells with all of my energy going to holding up my barrier. There was no way out.

The knife slammed down once more, draining away the last of my strength. Seeing my barrier falter, a sadistic smile crept over Sebastian's face. He slowly raised the knife overhead when the door to the room was slammed open with such force that it seemed like it might pop off its hinges.

In the doorway stood Lesti, a magical light hovering over her shoulder, "Air Blast!" Without missing a beat, she cast the very same spell that Sebastian had used on Oliver. However, the scale of the two spells was completely different. A ball of wind slammed into Sebastian so hard that he was sent flying into the far wall of the room. He would be lucky if he didn't have a few broken bones.

Lesti ran over and kneeled down, picking me up in her arms, "Astria! Are you okay? I got here as fast as I could!" She had made it just in time, and I had never been more thankful to see her.

"Don't worry. I'm fine, just a little groggy is all."

Lesti looked around the room, her eyes locking on Oliver lying on the floor, "What the heck is going on here?"

"I'll explain later, for now, we should probably go and get one of the Instructors."

"Alright, let's go grab Lani. She should be patrolling the grounds," Lesti stood up and started to walk toward the doorway. However, just as we were about to leave, an eerie purple glow began to illuminate the room behind us.

Summoning

Lesti turned around with me still in her arms. The magic circle on the floor was pulsing with a purple light. I could see magic being drawn in rapidly from Oliver, who lay on the far edge of the circle. With every passing second, the circle glowed brighter and brighter as it became more saturated with magical energy.

"What's going on? Who activated the circle?" I asked Lesti as I stared in shock. However, she didn't respond, staring at the circle intently instead. After a couple of seconds, her eyes grew wide, and I felt her body tense up before uttering a single word.

"Blood."

"Blood?" I looked up at Lesti, confused before looking back over at the circle. That was when I saw a small bit of blood on the floor beneath Oliver. He must have cut his head when Sebastian knocked him to the ground.

"We have to stop it! Aqua Sphere!" Lesti cast a spell without warning, sending a decently sized sphere of water flying toward the magic circle. However, as it approached, the magic holding the sphere together was absorbed into the circle. The water spread out splashing over the circle, but it wasn't concentrated enough to wash it away.

"Aqua Sphere!" Lesti attempted to cast the spell again, but most of the water in the room had just been thrown at the circle. Whenever her magic would attempt to get close to the circle to gather it back up, it would get absorbed, causing the circle to glow even brighter.

"Lesti, stop! It's just absorbing more of your magic!" I looked up at Lesti, who grit her teeth in frustration, "Hey, what's going on? Why are you panicking so much?"

"This circle, it's not right," Lesti took a deep breath and began to explain, "Several of the ruins are wrong, and others are missing. It took me a bit to read it, but I'm sure of it now. This isn't a familiar summoning circle anymore. It's something else, something twisted. I don't know what will show up if the ritual finishes at this point, but the binding ruin is missing, so whatever it is won't be bound to its summoner."

I stared at the circle for a moment before coming to a decision, "Lesti, leave me here and go find Frederick."

"What!? No. I'm not leaving you here. In your state, you'll be defenseless!"

"We don't have time to argue about this! We need to get help before the summoning finishes and can't leave Oliver and Sebastian here unconscious. Now, go!"

Lesti looked at me for a moment before carefully placing me on the ground. *Good. Now we can have Frederick call Skell up here if something really nasty comes out of the circle. I just need to figure out how I'm going to buy time. Maybe I can-.* My thoughts were stopped in their tracks as Lesti stepped in front of me.

"W-What are you doing? You're supposed to go get Frederick! Why are you standing there!?" I lost my cool and yelled at Lesti as I tried my best to gather some strength into my legs.

"I'm not leaving you here alone. Whatever comes out of that circle, we'll face it and beat it together," She glanced over her shoulder and grinned brightly at me, "After all, what good is all the hard work we both put in if we just run away at the first sign of danger?"

Despite all her bravado, I could see she was shaking slightly. I couldn't read the magic circle, but if it had Lesti this spooked, then something bad must be coming. That was probably why she didn't want to leave me here by myself. Still, if that was the case, I couldn't afford to let her fight on her own either.

I let out a heavy sigh, "Fine, have it your way. Don't say that I didn't warn you though," I used all of my willpower to force myself to my feet and walked to stand beside her, "That being said, I'm not just going to sit by and let you do this by yourself," I rubbed against her leg, "I'm here with you," She didn't respond, but her shaking stopped, and the forced grin on her face relaxed just a little.

I turned to watch the glowing circle with her. The eerie purple light that had filled the room was so bright now that it was hard to look at. Each time the light pulsed, I felt my stomach turn slightly as a feeling of light nausea passed over me. I braced myself for the moment when the summoning would finish, but just as I did, the light faded from the circle.

I started to relax a little and looked over at Lesti, "Did the summoning fail? Looks like we might have gotten lucky, huh? What are the odds the spell would f-"

Before I could finish my sentence, I saw dark sickening looking tendrils of magic burst forth from the magic circle. They swelled toward the air above the center of the circle and acted like they were grabbing hold of something that I couldn't see. Before I even had a moment to think about what was happening, the tendrils of magic tore the fabric of the world asunder before us.

A rift appeared above the magic circle, and a shock wave of magical energy rushed forth from the other side. However, unlike the magical energy that I was used to seeing, this was a dark, sickly purple color. The energy passed through us, and I immediately felt sick.

The nausea I had felt when the magic circle had been pulsing couldn't even compare to what I felt now. The energy that had just passed through us was disgusting and impure in a way that I hadn't ever experienced. Just coming in contact with it made me feel like there were a million cockroaches crawling over my body. I started retching involuntarily as the rift before us grew wider.

Beside me, Lesti wasn't faring any better. She had turned away and was dumping the contents of her dinner onto the stone floor. Her face was pale, and she was sweating slightly. Once her stomach was finally empty, she turned back to face the magic circle, her breathing heavy and ragged.

What the hell is going on? I stared at the rift before us. It had stopped growing and continued to expel the disgusting magical energy that was making Lesti and myself ill. The inside of the rift looked like it was filled with some sort of purple ooze.

Then from that very same ooze, a single hand burst forth. In many regards, it looked like a human hand, except it was gray, and the fingers were long and tipped with razor-sharp claws. It sat there, suspended in mid-air with purple ooze dripping to the floor for a moment. Then, it reached over and grabbed the edge of the rift and began to pull whatever was attached out.

Slowly, more and more of the creature emerged from the rift as it pulled itself free of the ooze. I knew that we should probably attack while it was pulling itself free, but neither of us could focus with all the disgusting magical energy floating around. Before we could do anything, the creature emerged entirely and tumbled to its knees on the floor in front of the rift before slowly rising to its feet.

As it stood, I was finally able to get a good look at its features. It stood at just over seven-foot-tall and had long, thin limbs. Parts of its torso, forearms, and lower legs were covered in black fur while the rest of its body was an ashen gray. Its ears were long and pointed, and a pair of bat-like wings sprouted from its back.

Then, I saw the creature's face. At first glance, it appeared to be that of a normal, albeit gaunt, man. However, when I looked closer, I could see that it had razor-sharp rows of teeth filling its mouth. Its eyes were the most disturbing part of the whole creature, though. They were large orbs that were entirely jet black and had no pupils. Looking into them was like peering into an abyss from which not even light could escape.

The monster before us finally reached its full height. Standing upright, its head nearly brushed against the ceiling. Rearing its head back, it opened its mouth wide and let out a high-pitched shriek. The sound was so loud that it felt like it would break my eardrums. Lesti covered her ears with her hands, and my own ears folded down against my head instinctively.

As the creature's shriek continued, the disgusting magic that had permeated the room began to flow into it. It rushed towards the monstrosity faster and faster until all of it had been absorbed. The nausea that I had felt since the creature appeared started to lessen. At the same time, the creature continued to absorb magic from the rift as it slowly grew smaller and smaller.

SUMMONING

Soon, the rift knitted itself shut, and the creature's shrieking stopped. A high-pitched sigh escaped the creature's mouth as it slowly turned its head to look around the room. Lesti and I braced for an imminent attack, but instead, it started speaking in a sickening high-pitched voice.

"Ah, the mortal realm. It really has been too long," it took a deep breath and grimaced, "The air is just as foul as I remember. Oh well, that can be fixed easily enough once I've taken my seat of power."

The creature then turned its empty gaze to us, "Oh, a human mage and her familiar. Not much of a welcoming party, but no matter. Are you the ones who summoned me? If so, then I really must thank you. I was growing quite bored on the other side."

"As if I would summon a foul creature like you!" Lesti put on her toughest expression and shouted back at the creature, "Go back to where you came from, you lowly beast!"

"Kyihihi!" The creature let out a high-pitched laugh, "You're an interesting one, little girl. I haven't had anyone speak to me like that since that overgrown black lizard centuries ago."

Overgrown black lizard? He couldn't mean Skell, could he?

"Still, I do have to correct you," The creatures dropped its jovial expression and sneered at Lesti, "I'm no beast. I am the archdemon Thel'al. Soon, I will be ruling over this miserable world of yours, so you would do well to show me the proper respect."

"Archdemon!?" Lesti shouted out loud before silently reaching out to me, "Astria, if this thing is what he claims to be, then we might be in trouble. Archdemons are an even match for adult dragons!"

"Kyihihi! That's right but worry not, mortal girl. I am a kind soul," Thel'al ran his long, forked tongue across his razor-sharp teeth, "If you grovel sincerely enough, then I'll let your transgression slide with a small punishment. Yes, ripping off one or two of your limbs should suffice in that case. Kyihihi."

"Sorry, but that's not going to happen. I don't intend to grovel before anyone," Lesti took her ready stance, "Let me be the first to welcome you to our world though. Fireball!" Lesti produced a large fireball that raced toward Thel'al, striking the demon directly in the chest. Upon impact, a small explosion occurred, kicking up large amounts of dust and dirt.

While the demon's vision was obscured by the dust, Lesti reached down and picked me up, "We're running!"

"What!? We can't run! Oliver is still there!" I struggled to escape Lesti's grip. I couldn't just leave the boy there to his fate.

"Don't worry. The demon will follow us for sure after that," Lesti turned and started running toward the hall, "We need to get away from Oliver and Sebastian right now. I can't fight with my full strength while they're around."

So, she was holding back after all. I had noticed that Lesti's fireball didn't have its usual impact. Still, we couldn't just leave Oliver and Sebastian behind unprotected like that.

"Fine, but make sure that giggling freak follows us! I'll cover your rear," I stopped struggling, and Lesti broke free from the smoke and dust in the room and dashed out into the hall.

As we did, I felt a surge of magic behind us. Without looking back, I threw up the strongest magical barrier that I could. Thel'al burst forth from the cloud of dust and dirt in the classroom, his entire body wrapped in the sickening purple magical energy that had poured out of the rift. He must have been boosting his physical abilities with magic because he was on top of us in an instant.

He swung at us with his large clawed hand. It struck the barrier and smashed right through it, only slowing for a moment. Luckily, that little bit of time was enough to put some distance between us. Right as the blow hit the barrier, I cast a hastily modified Wind Rake spell on us, propelling us away from Thel'al. However, I miscalculated the force, and we crashed through the large window in the hallway and were sent tumbling to the ground below.

Just before we hit the ground, I used Air Walk to slow our momentum and direct us away from the building like a slide. Lesti tumbled to the ground with me still in her arms. We came to a stop about twenty feet away from the old annex building. Lesti was cut in a few places from when we had burst through the window, but other than that, she seemed to be fine.

I hopped out of her arms and stared up at the broken window. I still wasn't one hundred percent, but it seemed the worst of the sleeping drugs effects had worn off. Thel'al was standing in the window, staring down at us with an angry sneer on his face. Without a word, he leapt from the window down to the ground. A powerful flap of the wings on his back was enough to slow his momentum and allow him to touch down softly.

"Lesti, this guy is too fast for you to fight up close," I reached out to Lesti and began to cast Speed Boost and Power Cat silently, "I want you to leave the close-quarters combat to me and provide support from the rear, okay?"

Lesti cast a worried glance in my direction, "I can't say you're wrong, but are you going to be okay?"

"Yeah. I'll be fine. The drugs have mostly worn off at this point I think," I walked in front of Lesti and took a ready position, bearing my fangs at Thel'al, "Besides, I've got quite a bit of experience battling against overpowered monsters."

Thel'al glanced down at me, the look on his face shifting from one of anger to one of amusement, "Kyihihi. So, the little girl's familiar is going to be my opponent now? How quaint. Try to not to break right away little kitty, I need you to suffer a bit first, or else it's no fun. Kyihihi."

"Oh, don't worry. I won't," With that, I dashed toward Thel'al with all my might. I quickly closed the gap and found myself directly at his feet. Before he could react, I leapt up and struck him in the jaw with my claws fully extended. His head snapped back at the force of the blow, and deep cuts appeared under his jaw.

Just as I was about to continue pressing my attack, I felt another surge of disgusting magic. Spears of rock formed rapidly and launched themselves at me. I use Air Walk to gain a foothold and leapt back, putting some distance between us and dodging the projectiles.

Thel'al's head slowly raised back into the correct position with a loud snap. He dabbed at the cuts under his jaw, his hand coming away with drops of purple blood, "Oh, my. It seems I was rather careless. I didn't expect such a feeble little mage girl to have a high ranking familiar. Kyihihi. What a blunder," The carefree and amused expression disappeared from his face, once again replaced by one of anger.

"Still, to make me bleed deserves a punishment of the highest order. Death would be too kind for you," A sick and twisted smile came over his face, "Kyihihi. Yes, I know. Your punishment will be to watch helplessly as I torture your master to death! Yes, that will do nicely, Kyihihi."

"Like I'll let you!" I lunged at the archdemon's throat, but this time he was ready for me. He sidestepped my attack by pivoting on one foot. Continuing the motion, he spun around and brought a powerful backhand blow down on me from behind.

"Earth Wall!"

Lesti's shout echoed across the lawn, and a wall of earth sprung up between Thel'al and me. His hand crashed into the wall with enough force to cause it to crumble. However, it was enough to stop his momentum. I used Air Walk to gain a foothold and launched myself back at him.

With his momentum killed by the wall Thel'al's back was partially turned towards me. I decided to take advantage of this and aimed for the back of his neck. The archdemon was slow to react, and my fangs and claws came boring down on him. However, just before my claws could find purchase, he ducked down so fast it seemed like his spine might snap in half.

I went sailing straight past him and landed on the ground in front of Lesti, my feet digging into the earth to slow my momentum. Once again, my attack had failed to land a blow. This was going to be a problem. I was clearly slower than him. I could further boost my speed and power, but each time I did, the amount of time I would be able to fight was reduced.

"Lesti," I glanced back at the girl behind me, "Do you have any spells that you can use to slow him down?"

She shook her head, "I don't have any spells like that, but I can try and slow him down with attack spells."

"Alright, give him everything you've got. Don't hold anything back, got it?"

"What if you get caught up in the crossfire, though?" Lesti looked at me with a worried expression on her face.

"Don't worry," My tail twitched about mischievously as an idea started to form in my head, "I've got a plan for that. Just make sure you don't hold back and try to hit him from different angles if you can."

With the plan in place, I turned my full attention back to the demon before us. In the few seconds we had been forming our plan, he hadn't been standing by idly. Disgusting purple magic swirled around him as he cast a series of spells. A large number of earthen spears and fireballs took shape around him.

With a wave of his hand, he launched the projectiles at me, I dashed forward and used my speed to slip between the projectiles. However, instead of crashing into the ground harmlessly, each one that I dodged changed course and began to chase after me. Soon I had an entire swarm of fireballs and earth spears hounding me as I tried to make my way toward Thel'al.

Still, no matter how hard I tried, I just wasn't making any progress. Each time I would start moving towards him, I would be forced back by a wave of projectiles intercepting me. *What kind of crazy spell is this!? He's controlling each one so precisely and isn't even breaking a sweat.*

My mind flashed back to my training with Skell. Even though he had thrown countless spells at me, he had never controlled them this precisely. Still, there did seem to be one weakness to controlling spells this accurately. I had been watching Thel'al closely, and he hadn't been moving this entire time.

Based on the flow of magic I was seeing; he was adjusting the trajectory and speed of each projectile in real-time. The insane amount of concentration given the speed we were fighting at was enough to send a chill down my spine. The difference between us was nearly immeasurable in both power and experience. Still, the situation wasn't hopeless. After all, I wasn't alone.

"Fireball!"

A powerful ball of flame roared to life behind Thel'al. While he had been focused on me, Lesti had circled around behind him and was now launching a full-strength Fireball spell directly at him.

"Kyihihi. An ambush, is it? How amusing!"

Thel'al laughed, seemingly amused by our attempts to strike at him. He turned to face Lesti and deal with the threat of her spell. He must have thought that his spell would keep me busy long enough to deal with the fireball, but that was a mistake on his part.

As soon as he took his gaze off of me. I leapt into action. Using the techniques that Skell had taught me, I began using Spell Jamming to interfere with Thel'al's projectiles. I quickly redirected each of them and brought them all together into one large concentrated attack, which I sent flying at the archdemon from the opposite side of Lesti's attack.

At the same time, Lesti cast two consecutive Earth Wall spells on either side of Thel'al cutting off his escape routes. With powerful spells approaching him from either side and his movement restricted, he only had one way out. Thel'al jumped straight up just before the spells reached him. The two sets of spells collided, causing an explosion that shook the ground and broke the windows in the nearby buildings.

"Kyihihi!"

The archdemon looked down at the conflagration below and let out another high-pitched laugh. However, we weren't done yet. While all of this had been happening, I had pushed my Speed Boost and Power Cat spells to their limit and leapt above Thel'al.

I pushed off a foothold I had created with Air Walk and came crashing down on the archdemon's head like I had been shot out of a cannon. Caught unaware, he wasn't able to dodge in time, and I smashed into the back of his skull with all of my might. There was a sickening thud, and he was sent crashing down into the burning earth below.

He struck the ground with enough force to kick up a large cloud of dust and dirt. I used Air Walk to redirect myself over to Lesti's side. As I landed, I felt my legs buckle as exhaustion washed over my body. The last of my magic had been exhausted by my reckless use of Speed Boost and Power Cat.

"Do you think that did it?" Lesti asked me without taking her eyes off the smoke and dust.

"I sure hope so. I'm completely out of gas at this point."

We both stared at the smoking crater before us, waiting to see if the archdemon Thel'al would emerge.

Despair and Vows

In the nearby dorms, students had started to come out of their rooms to see what was happening, drawn out by the noise of our fighting. They peered out at the lawn through the shattered windows. I could hear scared murmurs as they saw the carnage that had unfolded.

With my keen hearing, I could tell that the prevailing rumor was that this was a fight between two students. Some of the third years were even suggesting they go investigate and make sure no one was hurt. *I have to stop them. If any of them come out here, they'll be in danger. Guess I finally get to talk with the other students.*

"Everyone, stay inside the dorms," I projected my thoughts as far as I could, "There's a dangerous intruder on the school grounds."

"Hey, did you hear that? Like, a voice inside your head?"

"You heard it too? Who was that?"

"They say there's an intruder! What do we do!?"

Unfortunately, it appeared my attempt to keep everyone inside the dorms was backfiring and causing more confusion. None of the students knew my voice. I started to worry that they wouldn't listen to me and would wander out of the dorms, but that worry was nipped in the bud in the next moment.

A surge of sickening magical power erupted from the center of the smoldering crater before us. The slight feeling of nausea returned as the energy hit me. At the same time, the force of the magic blew away all of the smoke and dust, revealing Thel'al standing in the center. He was covered in shallow cuts and was burned in a few places, but none of his injuries appeared to be serious.

The clamoring students fell silent as they saw the archdemon for the first time. Several of them resorted to vomiting up their dinner as the wave of magic hit them. Perhaps we had gained a bit of an immunity to it after being exposed for so long earlier. I didn't feel nearly as nauseous as I did in the old annex building.

"Kyihihi!" Thel'al let out his loudest laugh yet and flashed his dagger filled smile at us, "It seems I've taken the both of you too lightly. I guess I'll have to get just a little more serious after all. Kyihihi!"

Suddenly, the magic that had been flowing out of Thel'al since the beginning of our fight doubled in output. It was now flowing out of him so quickly that it looked as though he was wreathed in a dark aura. This aura alone was enough to make some of the students in the main building lose consciousness. Those were the lucky ones. Anyone who was left standing was reduced to a retching, heaving mess. I could feel my own stomach start to turn over, but the fear and adrenaline kept me from getting sick.

Thel'al dashed towards us even faster than before. Dirt and rocks were thrown into the air with each step that he took. "Fireball!" Lesti fired a powerful ball of fire at the charging demon, but there was no way that was going to work now. Before the flames could even get close to him, he moved out of the way of the spell.

"Kyihihi! You're far too slow little mage-"

Boom!

There was an explosion as the fireball crashed into Thel'al. The demon was shoved backward several feet, and a few more burns appeared on his body. He stared at us with a stunned expression. *Well, I guess I can't blame him for that. As far as he can tell, Lesti just changed the direction of her spell at the last minute. I highly doubt he thought any human mage could pull that off, much less a little girl.*

Lesti, for her part, was doing a pretty good job of keeping a solid poker face on.

"Astria, what was that?"

"Just a little trick I learned from my teacher," I glanced up at her as my tail swished back and forth mischievously, "Keep peppering him with fireballs.

I'll make sure to keep him on his toes."

Lesti nodded and started firing off fireball after fireball. Each time she did, I would wait until the spell was close to Thel'al or in one of his blind spots, then I would use spell jamming to redirect the spell back at him. The archdemon continued to try and approach us, but between Lesti's continuous attacks and my tricky redirections, we were managing to hold him at bay.

"Kyiaaa!" Thel'al let out a high-pitched shriek of rage as another redirected fireball cut off his path, "I've had enough of you pests!"

The archdemon's magic surged as he began to cast a spell. Fireballs started to form in the air around him, growing in number by the second. Lesti continued to press her attack as he cast the spell, but each fireball she launched was intercepted by one of Thel'al's own.

Even though quite a few of them were being used to block our attacks, the number of fireballs in the air continued to grow to an absurd amount. At this point, there were so many that I could feel the heat despite the distance between us. Soon our vision was filled with nothing but fireballs and the demon himself.

"Fireball!" Lesti fired off one more shot. However, Thel'al didn't even bother to intercept this one. He simply batted it away with a backhanded swing of his arm. The fireball exploded on impact, but as the smoke cleared, it was obvious that there wasn't any damage. The spell had been too weak.

Lesti fell to a knee as she finally reached the limits of her magical power, "Sorry. Seems like I'm at my limit."

I rubbed against her, "Don't apologize. You did great," I stepped in front of Lesti and took a deep breath.

"Kyihihi. Fighting to the last, I see. Excellent!" Thel'al ran his tongue across his sharp teeth, "Keep fighting until the moment when you lose all hope! I can't wait to see the look on your face once you realize that all is lost, that you have lost! Kyihihi!" He raised one long arm before him, "Now, die!"

Several of the fireballs shot toward us at once. I used spell jamming to redirect each one of them around us. However, by the time I had finished with those, the next wave was already on its way. As I continued to redirect the balls of fire, I started to believe I could defend against this monstrous attack.

That was when I noticed something wasn't right. Despite how many of the fireballs I had already redirected, it didn't seem like the total number had gone down at all. I watched carefully as the next few attacks were launched, and what I saw nearly broke my will. Each time a fireball was sent toward us, another one would immediately form to take its place.

I came to a hard realization. *He's toying with us and has been this whole time.* I thought back to our fight up until this point. From the beginning, I had known that he was strong. His body enhancement spells alone were enough to tell me that. However, each time we had pushed him, he had shown us a new level of strength.

The confidence I had been feeling before started to crumble. Every attack I had to deflect felt heavier and seemed to come faster than ever. My breathing became ragged, and my heart began to beat wildly. I felt unsteady on my feet as my legs began to tremble. On top of all that, my vision began to blur around the edges.

Did he cast some sort of spell on me? What is happening? My mind flashed back to my old life. The entire time, I had lived in the comfort and safety of the modern world. Across both my lives, the scariest thing that had ever happened to me was getting lost in the store as a child. I had never had to fight for anything, much less my life. For the first time since I had come to this world, I felt threatened. *I'm scared. There's no way I can beat a monster like this.*

"Kyihihi! Yes! Yes!" Thel'al pointed at me with a thrilled smile on his face, "That's the expression I wanted to see! Now, die as you curse your own weakness!"

Another series of fireballs flew toward us, but I didn't reflect them this time. *I can't do this. There's just no way I can beat him.* My body froze as the terror and despair took over. I stared at the ground in front of me, waiting for the inevitable to come.

"Earth Wall!" Lesti dashed in front of me and cast her spell. A towering wall of dirt and rocks formed before us at the last second. The earth shook as a series of explosions blasted the wall to bits. Lesti panted heavily as fatigue from overusing her magic began to set in but looked back at me with a cheerful smile.

"Looks like you need a break. Don't worry. I'll hold him off until you recover, so take your time."

I stared back at her in disbelief, "Why? You have to know we can't win, right? Why haven't you given up yet?"

"The odds have been stacked against me ever since I came to the academy," Lesti turned back to face Thel'al, "Someday, I'll have to face down the entire alliance and all of history behind it. What's a single archdemon compared to that?"

"Lesti, you…"

I stared at her back in disbelief and awe. When I had first met her, she had barely any power of her own and pushed herself so hard she had collapsed. Yet, despite all that, she had never given up. She had worked hard and became stronger than any of her classmates.

"Besides, I can't go breaking my vow."

"Vow? What do you…" My mind flashed back to the day I arrived in this world. On that day, Lesti had made me her familiar and had vowed to protect me, keep me safe, and show me a world that no one else could or die trying.

My shaking stopped, and my breathing returned to normal. *You crazy girl. Why would you go that far for me? Why would you make a crazy vow like that to someone that you had just met? And you plan on keeping it, even though I've barely done anything for you?*

Another wave of fireballs, even larger than the last, flew toward us. Lesti fired her own fireballs off in an attempt to intercept them, but there were too many, and Lesti's magic was too depleted. Still, she continued to fire shot after shot, even as the flames closed in around her.

A single fireball broke past Lesti's defense. *Alright, if that's the case, then there's only one thing I can do.* I steeled my resolve and leapt in front of Lesti, deflecting the ball of flame just wide. It was so close that it felt like it would actually burn me. Still, more fireballs continued to break through, and I continued to deflect them.

As we stood there on the edge of despair, barely holding off our own demise, my mind flashed back to the day I was summoned. Right after Lesti had finished her vow, Lani had burst into the room. With her vow, Lesti had offered me so much, but I had offered her nothing in return. Despite that, here she was fighting tooth and nail to keep her promise.

I began to recite the words that I should have said that day aloud for all to hear, "Lesti, I recognize you, with your burning spirit, as my master," For reasons I didn't understand, I felt magic power begin to well up from within me. I began to push back against the wave of fireballs bearing down on us, deflecting them faster and faster. In response, Thel'al increased the speed at which he launched them.

"I vow to protect you on whatever path you may take in this world. No matter what dangers or hardships stand in our way, I will break through them and create a path for you or die trying," As my vow neared its end, the magic within me reached a crescendo. I batted fireballs out of the sky as if they were mere flies, "I swear this on the name you have given me, Astria!"

The image of the magic circle from the day I was summoned flashed through my mind and appeared on the ground below us. At the same time, I felt something deep within my soul come free, almost as if a dam had burst. Magic power surged through me like a raging river.

"Kyi!? Summoning magic!?" Thel'al's composure crumbled at the sight of the magic circle beneath our feet, "What trickery is this!? A familiar can't perform a summoning!"

The magic circle flashed brightly and faded into nothingness, but the surge of magic that I had felt remained. Thel'al seemed to think we were a threat now. Every fireball that had been hanging in the air around him surged toward us at once. There was no escaping or diverting such a large-scale attack, we would still be caught up in the explosion.

I guess this is as good a time as any to give it a shot! I felt as though I would explode if I didn't outlet some of the power that now flowed through me, so I did just that. I focused my vision, paying close attention to the magic that held the Fireball spells together. Then, I unleashed the wave of power flowing through me.

Tendrils of glowing magical energy rushed forth from my body with only one purpose, to unwind the magic holding the Fireball spells before me. My magic reached the fireballs and started to work on the magical energy that bound the spells together. Thel'al's eyes widened as he felt his spells start to come undone. He tried to resist, but I overwhelmed him with the sheer amount of magic I dumped into my task.

Still, the fireballs continued to surge toward us. Behind me, Lesti widened her stance and grit her teeth as she prepared to cast a defensive spell. Then, all at once, I completed my work and the wall of fire that had threatened to take our lives, dissipated into a puff of hot air. Orange and red sparks filled the air like little fire spirits as the last of the flames faded to nothing. It would have been beautiful, given any other circumstance.

Thel'al stared at me dumbstruck, unable to process what had just happened. I didn't waste a single second. Casting Speed Boost and Power Cat at maximum power, I transformed into my tiger form and rushed toward the archdemon.

I was on him in an instant. The powerful jaws of an adult tiger bit into his shoulder as my full weight slammed him into the ground. Blood spurted out of his mouth as he slammed into the ground, and a look of shock and fear formed on his face.

I continued to bite and claw at Thel'al. For his part, he tried to use spells to knock me off, but I used spell jamming each time to cancel them. The archdemon was forced to use his long arms to protect his vitals. Purple blood coated my fur and flew through the air as I reduced them to a bloody mess.

"Kyiii! Curse you! Curse you! Curse you!" Thel'al screamed at me as his panic reached its peak. He lashed out at me with spell after spell, all of which I canceled. Not knowing how long this new power of mine would last, I tried to finish the archdemon off quickly

I slipped my head under his arms and aimed for the neck in an attempt to land the killing blow. However, in my haste, I hadn't properly pinned him down. As I shifted my weight forward, he wrapped his arms around my neck and put his feet on my stomach. Using my momentum and his insane strength, the demon pulled me wide of my target and sent me tumbling off of him.

"I won't let you escape!"

Eager to press my advantage, I jumped to my feet and made to lunge at Thel'al before he could recover. However, just as I did, I felt a sharp pain deep in my chest. The magic that had been surging within me suddenly stopped, almost as if someone had suddenly turned off the faucet. My tiger transformation failed, and I was left standing only a few feet from a bloodied and angry archdemon.

No, no, no! Come on magic, you can't give out on me now! I pleaded with everything that I had to try and get the surge of magic that had been flowing through me to return. Yet, no matter how hard I begged or pleaded, it was gone. *Why does this always happen at the worst time!?*

Thel'al stood and turned to face me. Purple blood dripped off his arms onto the ground. The passive expression on his face sent a chill down my spine. Up until this point, he had been playing with us. Slowly he had ramped up his power in an attempt to break our spirits, but now that was all done. He took a heavy step toward me.

"Fireball!" Lesti launched a fireball toward the demon's back. Without ever taking his eyes off me, Thel'al swung his long arm back and swatted the ball of flame aside. I scuttled backward, trying to get away but soon found myself backed up against the smoldering crater created by our earlier attack.

Thel'al continued to approach me until he was just out of range to grab me. At this close of a range, I could see that the wounds on his arms had already healed over, forming dark purple scars. Seeing how quickly he had healed increased my panic further. Whether it was some innate ability of demons or he had used magic, it showed that I had missed my chance.

He held one arm out, his palm facing toward me, without saying a word. I saw the dark magic energy begin to swirl in his hand, and a fireball started to form. I tried to use spell jamming to stop the spell, but I didn't have enough strength left to overpower him.

The ball of flame grew larger and brighter with each passing moment. It must have been only a second, but it felt like an eternity watching the spell come together. It was if time had slowed to a fraction of its usual speed. My heart pounded wildly in my chest, but my body didn't lock up. I threw up my best magical shield and closed my eyes, waiting for the fire to consume me.

"Astria!" I could hear Lesti yelling at me from across the lawn, her voice filled with emotion.

"Sorry, Lesti looks like I wasn't able to protect you after all. Thanks for everything."

"No!" she gave one last shout as Thel'al released his spell.

Boom!

The explosion I had been waiting for finally came. I waited for my shield to break and the unimaginable pain of being burned to ash to overtake me, but that moment never came. *Am I dead again? Maybe the flames burned me so fast that I just didn't feel anything?*

"Closing your eyes with an enemy right in front of you?" A familiar voice snapped me out of my delusions. I opened my eyes to find Frederick standing before me, "It seems Skell was lax in your training after all."

I looked around to find that the ground before me burned deeply. Thel'al had been blown back several feet and had taken to the air. Across the grounds, Lani was holding Lesti back as she struggled to break free and run over to me, tears streaming down her face.

I looked up at the Frederick as my tail swished back in forth in agitation, "You sure took your sweet time. What the hell took you so long, huh!?"

"That's a rather ungrateful tone to take with someone who just saved your life." Frederick responded without ever taking his eyes off of Thel'al, "I came as fast as soon as Lania arrived in my office. Well, once I was able to get her to stop blabbering incoherently anyway."

"Did you get lost or something!? We've been fighting for ages over here! Did you not hear the explosions!?"

"Ages? Your inexperience is showing little one. You've only been fighting for a few minutes."

"A few minutes? That can't be…" I reflected back on our fight up until this point and realized he was right. All of the adrenaline had warped my sense of time, making the whole fight feel longer than it actually was.

"Still, I'm impressed you've managed to last this long against an archdemon. It seems having Skell train you wasn't a total waste," For the first time since I had met him, Frederick's voice took on a softer tone, "You did well. I'll take over from here."

"Kyiii! Curse you! Curse you! Curse you!" Thel'al gnashed his teeth and clawed at this face as he hung in the sky, "Why won't you die, you cursed animal!?"

"Silence demon," Frederick held his hand in front of him and launched a fireball at the archdemon. Thel'al swung his arm in an attempt to swat away the fireball, but it exploded on impact.

"Kyiii! It burns!" The hand that he had used to swat the fireball was charred black. He glared at Frederick with hatred in his eyes, "How is this possible!? How can a mere human burn me so badly!?"

"Mere human?" Frederick turned the back of his hand to face Thel'al, " I'm no mere human, you demon scum. I am the flame that purifies our world of foul creatures such as yourself, leader of the Alandrian Alliance Special Subjugation Force, Frederick Grestin!"

Thel'al's went wide at seeing the mark on the back of Frederick's hand, "That mark! Kyihihi! I see! I see! It all makes sense now! So, that impudent wyrmling still lives! Oh, how the mighty have fallen, being bound to a weak little human, like yourself."

Frederick lowered his hand and stared back at the Thel'al with a new intensity, "You know Skell? Just who are you, demon?"

Thel'al bowed with a flourish, his burnt hand clutched close to his chest, "Unfortunately, I'm afraid introductions will have to wait. It appears I have overstayed my welcome on this day. Kyihihi! I'll be taking my leave now."

"You're not going anywhere!" Frederick raised his hand once more and began to prepare a spell.

"Oh, are you sure you have time to be worrying about me right now?" The archdemon prodded Frederick throwing a sideways glance at the boys' dorm, "Your precious younglings are in danger, you know?"

Frederick and I both turned to look at the boys' dorm. Without us realizing it, a swarm of fireballs had formed in the sky above the dorm. Frederick immediately jumped into action, sweeping me up in his arms and dashing toward the boys' dorm. As I looked back over his shoulder, I saw a twisted smile form on Thel'al's face. Another swarm of fireballs began to form over the girls' dorm.

"Frederick! The girls' dorm!" I shouted a warning to Frederick.

"Don't worry. I know. He'll take care of it."

With a quick gesture from Thel'al, the fireballs plummeted from the sky towards both dorms at the same time. Frederick leapt up to the boys' dorm and began weaving a magical barrier spell, much like the one that Skell had taught me. However, the scale and strength were far superior to anything I had ever produced.

As the fireballs continued to descend, I looked over at the girl's dorm in a panic. Just as I did, an earth-shaking roar rang out from far below ground. Massive amounts of magical energy surged up from the ground below the girls' dorm and began forming the same barrier that Frederick had formed above the boys' dorm.

The fireballs slammed into both barriers at the same time, the explosions shook the buildings and filled the sky with smoke, but the barriers didn't so much as waver. After a few seconds, the barrage stopped, but Frederick didn't drop his barrier right away. He stared at the smoke covered sky cautiously, wary of another attack from the archdemon.

"Tch," Frederick clicked his tongue and lowered the barrier, "Looks like he escaped."

I wondered how he could be so sure with so much smoke in the sky. Then the realization hit me. There was too much smoke in the sky. None of the previous fireballs Thel'al had created had caused this much smoke. He had intentionally modified the spell to create a smokescreen to cover his escape. After a few minutes, the smoke finally cleared. Just as Frederick had said, Thel'al was gone without a trace.

Results

A glowing light flitted between Skell and me. The dragon and I sat in the very same cave where my training had taken place not long ago. After fighting for my life against Thel'al, the beauty of this cave was even more apparent to me. For a moment, I stared at the stalactites as they sparkled from the many magical lights floating by them.

A week had passed since our battle with Thel'al, and things were finally getting back to normal at the academy. The damage to the dorms and the grounds was mostly repaired, though I wasn't sure if the grass would ever be the same. All of the students had gone back to their normal routines just two days later.

The day after the battle, Lesti and I had been interviewed about what had happened to the point of exhaustion by the headmistress and a procession of instructors. After that, we had taken the next few days to rest and recover. Despite coming out of the fight largely unscathed, we had both been exhausted. As soon as we recovered, Lesti had gone straight back to studying for the practical exam, which had taken place yesterday.

"It's a miracle you're alive to tell me this story, little one," Skell's voice snapped me out of my reverie.

Today, I had finally made some time to come and talk to Skell about what had happened. Honestly, he had been the first person I had wanted to talk to, but after the interview marathon from hell, I didn't have the energy to come all the way down to the cave. I had finished my tale just before this. Skell had quietly listened the entire time and had only just now spoken.

"An archdemon is not a foe that any ordinary mage or familiar could face down. Even when facing strong opponents, they find ways to break their spirit. Thel'al, especially, enjoys wearing down his opponents in this manner."

"You seem awfully familiar with Thel'al, and he seemed to know about you as well," I narrowed my eyes as I stared at Skell, "He called you a wyrmling and seemed surprised that you were still alive. Care to tell me what's going on there?"

Skell turned and stared into the nearby water for a moment with a distant looking gaze, "I once battled Thel'al many years ago. Though I was victorious, I was severely wounded. Still, that is a tale for another time. For now, I would like to hear more about this surge of magical power that you spoke of."

"I pretty much told you everything I know," I cocked my head to the side and tried to recall any details I had missed before, "I was about to give up when Lesti reminded me of her vow, then the magic circle showed up under my feet. Once that happened, I felt a surge of magical power, which, of course, ran out at the worst time."

I swatted at a nearby rock as I remembered the moment when my newfound power had suddenly disappeared. Not paying attention to my surroundings, I smacked it right into a nearby stone. The small rock bounced off the stone and came back to hit me square in the chest before falling to the ground. There wasn't any real pain, but the rock hitting me in the chest caused me to pause.

"Actually, there is something I forgot," I walked over to the water's edge and stared at the spot where the rock had hit me, "Right before my magic cut out, there was a sharp pain in my chest. I didn't think much of it at the time, but do you think it was related?" I looked over at Skell to see his reaction.

The dragon closed his eyes in thought for a moment before nodding, "I suspect the two are most likely related. However, there is still one piece of the puzzle missing. You said that the magic circle that formed under you and the girl was the same one that was used to summon you, correct?"

"Yeah. That's right."

"Are you sure that nothing else happened right before that?" Skell stared at me intently.

I had avoided telling Skell about the vow I had made to Lesti. If I was still in human form, I would have blushed. *That was so embarrassing! What was I thinking spouting stuff like that!?* I wriggled in discomfort at the mere thought of the things I had said.!? Glancing over at Skell, I saw that he was now staring at me with a deadpan expression.

"W-Well, there was just one thing, but I really don't think it's that important..." I kept my glance firmly to the side as I did my best to gloss over the subject.

However, Skell wasn't going to let me escape so easily, "I'll be the judge of that. Now, tell me exactly what happened."

A few minutes later, I was doing my best ostrich impression trying to bury my head in the sand. Unfortunately, the floor was stone, so I just ended up mashing my face against the ground. I had done my best to avoid having to tell Skell about my vow, but he wasn't having any of that. *I can't believe he forced me to recite the entire thing!* The whole situation was made even worse by the occasional chuckle that found its way out of the dragon's throat.

"Ahem," Skell cleared his throat to get my attention. I turned to face him, tears still in the corners of my eyes.

"What is it? You want to embarrass me even more?"

"Oh, stop acting so pitiful. The vows made during a summoning are an important part of the ritual magic. The strength of your vow actually has an effect on the spell, you know."

"It does?" I peeled my face off the ground and looked up at Skell properly, "Why would summoning magic activate during the battle, though? I was summoned quite some time ago."

"That's because the summoning ritual was incomplete. When you were summoned, Lesti must have made a vow as part of the ritual, correct?"

"Yeah. That's right," I thought back to my summoning, "Then, right after that, Lani burst through the door, and the spell ended."

"Yes. That, right there, is the issue. You see, Astria, summoning magic isn't a one-way street. You can bind a familiar to your service, but unless that familiar agrees with the contract, then the spell will remain incomplete."

"If that's the case, then why didn't Lesti say anything?"

Skell shrugged his shoulders, "It's likely she didn't know, or perhaps she didn't want to pressure you into finalizing the contract."

"That does sound like something she would do. Still, if the contract being completed was where all of that power came from, then why did it suddenly stop?"

"Magical overload. It's a safety mechanism that prevents damage to your soul," Skell picked up a rock and used magic to surround it in flames, "Imagine this rock as your soul and the flames as the magic that it produces. Right now, the rock is safe because the flames are at a temperature the rock can handle."

"Alright, I'm following so far." I moved a little closer to Skell to get a better look at his demo.

"Now, if the amount or the quality of the magic being produced were to suddenly spike," Skell manipulated the flames, making them larger and hotter. So hot, in fact, that the rock underneath started to melt, "Then the soul becomes at risk of being damaged. In order to prevent this, the flow of magical energy gets shut off."

The rock fell to the floor with a thud as Skell released his magic, "This is what we call magical overload. It most likely happened because the amount and quality of your magic increased so suddenly, and your soul didn't have time to get used to it."

"So, basically, you're saying that I got too strong too fast, and my soul put a sort of limiter on so I wouldn't hurt myself?" Skell gave an emphatic nod at my explanation, but I wasn't the least bit please, "I almost died because of that stupid limiter! What kind of safety measure kicks in at a time like that!?"

Skell looked at me as though I had just said the most insane thing, "I don't think you understand little one. Even slight damage to the soul can have catastrophic effects. At best, you might lose your ability to use magic, and in the worst-case scenario, you would become an empty husk."

"I see," A shiver ran up my spine as I realized how much danger I had been in, "Still, there must be some way to fix it right? Like some sort of therapy?"

Skell shook his head, "Once the soul is damaged, it cannot be repaired by any means in the known world. That's why you must be careful. Forcefully pushing through a magical overload is as good as a death sentence."

"Right. No taking the limiter off. Got it."

Dong! Dong!

From far above ground, the sound of a large bell being rung echoed through the ground.

"Looks like it's time for you to take your leave," Skell brought his face down close to mine, "Be careful out there little one, Thel'al will be looking for a chance to strike back at you. He's not the type to live and let live if you know what I mean."

If Thel'al made Skell, a fearsome dragon, this cautious, I was going to pay attention. I nodded to Skell and turned back toward the passage leading back to the school, "I'll be careful. You be safe too, teacher. I don't know about your past with that demon, but he remembers you."

Skell gave me a quick nod without saying a word. There was a far-off look in his eyes that worried me slightly, but there wasn't anything I could do about it at the moment. With one last look back at the dragon, I took off down the hall, on my way to meet Lesti.

* * *

I emerged from Frederick's office into the hall outside. It was unusually crowded today and for good reason. Today, the rankings from the practical exam would be revealed. The revealing of the rankings was apparently a big event here at the academy. All of the students would gather in the central courtyard where a large board with rankings for each year of students would be posted.

I made my way down the hall toward the entrance to the courtyard, following the flow of students and other familiars. However, the traffic soon came to a stop just outside the entrance to the courtyard. *Seriously? It's already this crowded!? Why don't they do this on the lawn?*

Seeing a gap, I started to squeeze my way through the crowd. I probably could have just used Air Walk to jump over the crowd, but I didn't want to draw that much attention to myself. I had already started getting stares around campus after the battle with Thel'al. Needless to say, the secret about me being a high-level familiar was out of the bag.

I weaved my way through the maze of feet, claws, and paws around me until I was deep into the crowd. Unfortunately, there were so many bodies around that it was difficult to get my bearings. If it wasn't for the sun shining down from above, I might not have even realized I had entered the courtyard. *Man, I'm never going to be able to find Lesti this way.*

I looked around for a way to escape the crowd. Nearby, I spotted the railing that went around the outer edges of the covered walkway in the courtyard. Weaving my way over to the railing, I jumped up on top of it. However, there was still no sign of Lesti, so I decided to go higher.

Using Air Walk, I leapt up onto the roof of the covered walkway. Apparently, I wasn't the only one who had this idea. Several flying familiars were staring down at the crowds from their perch on the roof. I slowly made my way across the roof as I peered down at the crowd looking for Lesti, feeling like a predator stalking her prey.

I was about to give up and just ask her where she was when I saw a flash of red hair bobbing around near the front. Lesti was standing on her toes and looking through the crowd, trying to find me. After a moment, she spotted me and started waving wildly.

"Astria! Over here!" Her mental shout rang through my head.

"Calm down. I see you."

I rolled my eyes at my overenthusiastic partner and started making my way across the roof. I circled around until I was on the other side of the giant board. Crouching down, I prepared myself to jump over to the board. I could have used Air Walk to make things easy, but this seemed like a fun challenge.

After judging the distance, I made the leap and landed square on my target. *Yes, nailed it!* I mentally patted myself on the back as I re-situated myself on the thin top of the board. Unfortunately, my celebration was premature. The cloth covering the board slipped under my feet, and I tumbled off the front of the board.

In my panic, I tried to grab onto anything I could to keep myself from falling. My claws dug into the white cloth, slowing my fall, but I was too heavy for it to stop my fall completely. Instead, I fell to the ground and was buried in the heavy white cloth as I pulled it down with me.

I struggled for a few moments to find my way out of the maze of white that surrounded me, kicking and tearing at the cloth in an attempt to pull myself free. Eventually, my head popped out into the light of day, and I took a deep breath of the crisp autumn air.

Then, a familiar chill shot down my spine. I looked over to the right of the board, where some of the faculty were standing to see Lani staring at me with an icy cold smile. Behind her, Frederick furrowed his brow at me, and the headmistress rubbed the bridge of her nose. Meanwhile, all the students stared at me with dumbfounded expressions.

"Ahaha, sorry about that!"

As quickly as possible, I pulled myself free and escaped into the Lesti's arms, my heart racing as images of the lecture Lani was sure to give me flitted through my mind. The headmistress let out a heavy sigh and walked over to where I had just fallen, pushing the cloth under the board.

"Well, normally, I would give a speech here about your hard work paying off and all of that. However, I doubt any of you will listen since the scores are already revealed, so I'll keep it short," she shot me a glare that could have made even the most powerful of mages wither before continuing.

"These scores show the progress you've made and where you stand amongst your peers. For those of you that have risen or maintained their ranks, congratulations. For the rest of you, use this as an opportunity to motivate yourselves to be better," There was a long pause as she looked out over the crowd of students, "Lastly, Ms. Vilia, please come to my office after this, won't you?"

"Y-Yes ma'am!" Lesti stood rigid, and a wave of giggles came from those nearby.

"Very good. Then, without further ado, I present to you the results of the Alandrian Central Magic Academy Autumn practical exam!"

With those final words, the headmistress stepped out of the way, and the students started scanning the board for their placements. Looking up at the board from Lesti's arms, I could see that the board was broken down into four columns. Each column was for students that were in the same year.

RESULTS

I was surprised by how many students there were in each year. I had always assumed that Lesti's class was the only one for kids her age, but it seems that wasn't the case. Based on the number of names on the board, there were probably around three to four classes per year.

I scanned the names of the second years looking for Lesti. My eyes naturally started from the bottom. Most of her classmates' names were at the very bottom. The only three that were missing were Lesti, Oliver, and Sebastian. About midway up the list, I found Sebastian's name. He wasn't here today because he was under house arrest, but he had been allowed to take the exam after he had recovered.

On the other hand, Oliver's name wasn't on the list at all. According to Lani, he wasn't cooperating with the investigation, so he had been barred from taking the exam. Still, seeing the difference in treatment between the two left a bitter taste in my mouth. It felt like Sebastian was getting off easy just because he was a noble.

At the very top of the list sat a familiar name. Alexander Bestroff, the boy who was overflowing with magical energy, was number one. Right below him, in the number two slot was Lesti. I looked up at her to see what her reaction was to being ranked second in her year.

What I was met with was an expression of pure disbelief. *Well, I guess that's to be expected. I'm sure she thought she would get first, after all. It's pretty ridiculous that Alexander was able to beat her when she's using instruction-based magic.*

"Lesti, don't let it get to you…" I spoke privately to Lesti, trying to cheer her up.

"I'm second," Lesti lowered her head, and then the next thing I knew, I was being tossed into the air as she shouted, "I'm second! Do you see, Astria!? I'm second in my whole year!" The smile on her face was the brightest I had ever seen.

She caught me as I fell back down and did a quick spin and pulled me close, "Thank you so much. I wouldn't have been able to do this without you."

"Don't mention it," I rubbed my cheek against hers, "We're partners after all, right?"

She stared at me for a second before breaking into an even bigger grin than before, "Yeah, that's right! Well then, partner, I hope you're ready for what comes next!"

"What comes next? What do you me-"

Before I could even finish responding, Lesti ran out in front of the crowd and started scanning it for someone. Soon her eyes fell upon a familiar boy. Lesti pointed her finger at him and called out his name.

"Alexander Bestroff!" a sea of faces turned to look at us, including the boy himself, "Don't go getting too comfortable in that top spot! Astria and I are going to steal it from you before you know it. By the time we graduate, I'll be known as the undisputed number one mage in our year!"

Alexander looked Lesti and me up and down with his blue eyes. Magic poured out of him just like it did on the first day I saw him.

"Lesti, was it? I'll commend you for taking the second spot this time around. However, let me be frank, you have no chance of taking the top spot from me," His eyes drifted down and locked onto me, "You already have a high level familiar as your companion and still couldn't beat me, despite me not having a familiar of my own,"

Alexander then spread his hands wide, gesturing to the crowd of students behind him, "Once the rest of the students receive their familiars, I suspect the gap between you and I will grow again, and you'll fall back to your former rank at the bottom of the class."

I looked up at Lesti, expecting her to lose her cool and snap back at Alexander, but instead, she was calm. Her eyes had the same hard, determined look that I had seen so many times when she had been practicing spells late at night. *Based on that look, I'd say this boy is in for a rude awakening in the near future.*

"Think whatever you like. The results will speak for themselves. Let's go, Astria. We don't have any more time to waste here."

Lesti turned on her heel and made for the exit behind the board. I jumped out of her arms to walk beside her. The sound of students chatting excitedly slowly faded as we made our way out into the hallway. Looking up at Lesti, I posed a simple question.

"So, how do you plan to beat someone who can beat you without using instruction-based magic or a familiar of his own?"

"Hehe," Lesti let a slight chuckle and clasped her hands behind her head, "I honestly have no idea. I'm sure if we keep working hard, we'll figure something out, right partner?"

I turned my head away, "Don't go expecting me to bail you out after you picked a fight all on your own like that. You'll have to figure this out on your own."

"Don't be that way! There's no way I'll be able to be Alexander on my own! Come one, please?" Lesti threw her best pleading look my way.

I threw a sideways glance at her, "Well, I guess since you asked so nicely, I can help just a bit. Try not to fall behind, though."

With that, I dashed off down the hallway with Lesti hot on my heels, laughing as she chased me. I didn't know where I was going or what awaited me in this crazy new world, but I knew that she would be right there with me the entire way. I was her familiar, after all.

Newsletter

Thank you for reading my book! If you enjoyed it, please consider leaving a review. Want to know more about the latest releases, giveaways, and other news? Sign up for my newsletter now!

https://ranobepress.com/newsletter-signup/

Artist Information

Yura's arts is talented freelance artist with a focus on anime-style illustrations. She is available to hire for both personal and commercial commissions and can be contacted via her Twitter.

Twitter
https://twitter.com/yura_s_arts

Made in the USA
Columbia, SC
17 November 2023